LUNA STATION
QUARTERLY

Issue 049 | March 2022

Editor-in-Chief
Jennifer Lyn Parsons

Editors
Katrina Carruth • Anna Catalano • Wanda Evans
Angelica Fyfe • Cathrin Hagey • Sarah Pauling • Cait Ryan
Carly Racklin • Shana Ross • Gô Shoemake
Bridget Siniakov • Margaret Stewart • Izzy Varju

LUNA STATION PRESS
NEW JERSEY

First Paperback Edition March 2022
ISBN: 978-1-949077-30-8

Luna Station Quarterly publishes short fiction on March 1st, June 1st,
September 1st, and December 1st. For more information and submission
guidelines, please visit our website at lunastationquarterly.com

For Luna Station Press

Creative Director - Tara Quinn Lindsey
Editor-in-Chief & Founder - Jennifer Lyn Parsons

 LUNA STATION PRESS

www.lunastationpress.com

CONTENTS

Editorial

Jennifer Lyn Parsons

Jennifer Lyn Parsons is a writer and senior software engineer. Currently, she enjoys writing fantasy stories about middle-aged people who aren't into the whole "going on a quest" thing but do it anyway. When not writing code or prose, she is also the editor-in-chief of the venerable Luna Station Quarterly. She finds joy in baseball, tea, discovering music new and old, and making analog things.

Sometimes as we're putting together an issue, there are themes that develop in the submissions we receive. It always appears to be spontaneous in the moment, though often later I've been made aware of some themed writing contest or another whose rejects make our way into our slush pile.

However, there are larger thematic cycles that occur in fiction, often influenced either directly or indirectly by the events of the day. As I was organizing the story summaries for Tara Lindsey, our Creative Director, to read through as a cheat sheet for writing the back cover copy, I was reminded of how many stories in this issue are centered around loneliness and loss.

Now, before you put this issue down, let me assure you that this does not mean there is no hope or lightness within these pages. Our talented authors have produced works of beauty and even humor that lighten the darkest tale and makes them all worth reading. That said, I would be remiss not to acknowledge that the events of the last couple of years are beginning to surface in the fiction that crosses my desk.

There is a thought out there that stories go in cycles, with dark following light following dark, depending on the mood of the day. For example, many of you will remember the influx of zombie stories across media in the early 2010s. Some think that explosion of dark, apocalyptic fiction was brought on by the exponential increase of social media at the time and some feeling that we were all becoming "zombified" by our phones. If that theory stands, then it is no wonder that we'll be seeing more dark works in the next few years.

Many authors, myself included, find writing to be an outlet, not just for general creativity, but also for working through various emotions. We often don't just write what we already know, we also write so that we *can* know. We write what we don't understand about ourselves and the world so that we can get a better grasp on things going on around us.

It goes without saying that lockdown was highly impactful to everyone, and now it seems that stories that were written during that period, or are influenced by it, are beginning to be sent out for publication. I see this as a good thing, a healthy part of the cycle of literature, and a way for us all to begin to truly process and heal from the isolation so many people have gone through (and are still going through) throughout the pandemic.

Yet, I don't want to limit the influence of these works. The majority of the stories we publish are not set in the consensus reality we all know and live in. These tales are fantasy and science fiction, which means that they touch upon the themes of loneliness, loss and isolation in ways that show how timeless these problems are to the human condition.

Long after we've moved on to whatever it is that comes next, these stories will be more than a snapshot of what it felt like to be isolated from friends and family during the 2020 pandemic lockdown. Be it on a marooned space station far in the future, a dry desert in a magical land where small gods wander in seek of worship, or a simple, otherwise normal home that houses a magical pair of glasses, whether together and alone, these stories show us the range of possibilities we all have available to us when dealing with difficulties. Most of all, they show us what it means to be human.

L S Q | 049

The Important Things

Lisa Fox

Melanie was home again.

She sat in her parents' kitchen, staring at her mother's faux roses resting on the table. Rooted in a dusty plastic vase, they'd been there as long as she could remember. Pink and white petals deceived, soft and shimmering from a distance but up-close, rough and flaking, not unlike herself since her mother died.

The clock's ticking narrated the passage of moments, each one pulling Melanie further from the life she'd taken for granted. She thrummed her fingers on the quilted red placemat, picking at the hardened gravy on its ruffle. She wondered if her mother had noticed it congealing all those months before, the last time she tidied the kitchen, or if she dismissed it as a chore that could wait for later.

The surety of *later* deceived, the ruse of a contented life.

Melanie waited in the quiet, alone. Assertions to her older sister Amanda that she'd help clean out their parents' home were met with eye-rolls and sighs. Two seasons had passed since Melanie last entered the house, despite her best intentions. The last time, she'd trudged through a mound of unshoveled snow to reach the threshold; now, a rich palate of dead leaves blanketed the ground.

Yet Melanie arrived mid-morning, as promised.

The battle between responsibility and grief roiled in Melanie's gut, undignified as a bar brawl. She had no excuse to avoid her childhood home, other than the paralysis that crept through her arm and her hand each time she attempted to slip the key into the lock, or the tears that blurred the weathered tan siding outside until it was unrecognizable.

A mausoleum, this place where Melanie had dreamt each childhood dream, where she spent summer nights cupping fireflies in her palms.

This time, Amanda left the door open for Melanie, the lock and latch blameless.

Hinges had creaked as Melanie pushed the thick oak door open. She stepped over the threshold and into the foyer, her breaths short as she inhaled the stagnant air. The house felt stale as a vault and smelled like moist cardboard. Silence hung heavy as words whispered at her mother's bedside vigil, obscuring the light echoes of memory that childhood homes were supposed to maintain. It reminded Melanie of all she'd lost—first her father, then her mother—and why she wanted to be anywhere but in that house.

Half-filled boxes and bulging trash bags cluttered each room. Dark dust squares lingered on the walls, like the outlines of fallen bodies, where frames once hung. Her parents' wedding photo, where their story began. Baby and school portraits, an etched timeline of nuanced distinctions that the years bring as childhood slinks by—a bit like life, over when it's too late to appreciate it. All removed in Amanda's "progress."

Was nothing sacred to her sister?

But the kitchen remained mostly untouched. Colorful magnets still clung to the refrigerator, emergency phone numbers secured by the shining memento of Mom and Dad's 50th anniversary cruise and medication lists held by a smiling Mickey Mouse from their last Disney trip–the last vacation everyone took together. Among them, old photos hung, vibrance lost under decades of morning sunlight streaming through the window—Grandma Lane, Mom's mother, posing in front of a vintage car in a polka-dot dress, wearing tight curls and cat-eye shaped glasses; Dad kissing Mom underneath the Christmas mistletoe as Amanda and Melanie looked on, clad in footed pajamas. These artifacts blended into the backdrop of life, unnoticed but ever-present.

Melanie's phone pinged, a text from Amanda: *Running late. Start sorting kitchen. Luv ya!* It was just like her sister to pull that tough-love act. Amanda always baited the toughest tasks with a false lure of handholding and baby-steps, and, without fail, Melanie grabbed on to the pinch of her shiny hook. Under this guise, she'd learned to swim, to ride a bike. To survive her first teen breakup. It was how she put one foot in front of the other in the weeks after they'd lost Dad. How she got out of bed each day after Mom died.

Grasping the arms of the chair, Melanie stood and cleared her throat, as if announcing her presence to the silence. She glanced around the kitchen, wondering how to dismantle this room without rupturing the foundation of memories it supported. It was impossible to maintain the full mosaic that time had crafted in this kitchen, intricate as the custom backsplash Dad installed so many years ago. But how do you lift away and keep the most beautiful tiles without cracking through the wall?

***

The clock ticked forward with the progression of day, the roar of morning tamed to the whisper of late afternoon. Around her, items lay sorted: table linens, pots and pans, utensils and dishes, all evicted from decades-old dwelling places. Melanie spent the hours organizing–*compartmentalizing, it was what she was best at*–though she hadn't discarded a thing. She opened the refrigerator, grateful for the bottled waters Amanda left for them.

Sitting, Melanie took a swig, silently cursing her sister for leaving her alone in the house. She surveyed her progress–all that remained was the junk drawer. 'Chaos in a box,' her mother used to call it. The place for important, yet abandoned, things.

Six flashlights. Two fistfuls of paper clips. An empty tape dispenser. A corkscrew. Enough rubber bands to weave into a small, multi-colored ball. As Melanie bounced her newly crafted toy against the floor–*bounce, catch, bounce, catch*–she noticed a hint of shimmering gold peeking out through the latex gloves and empty pill bottles that still littered the drawer. She palmed the ball with her left hand, and with her right, fished through the mess and retrieved an old-fashioned eyeglass case from the back.

She stroked the sparkly casing, fingers tingling as her touch awakened a sprinkling of its remaining decorative glitter. Melanie couldn't remember the last time she had seen this case. Yet, she beheld it as she would an old friend whose smile transcends time and age. The rusted hinges protested as she snapped it open. Resting inside on a bed of faded red satin were Grandma Lane's glasses, the same ones worn in the photograph tacked to the refrigerator. Pearls and rhinestones adorned the corners of the pointed frames–the smooth plastic the color of apple-juice. Melanie removed them from the case and brought them to the refrigerator, holding them up next to the picture.

Melanie was ten when her grandmother died; Grandma Lane's was the first funeral she'd ever attended.

Why had Mom kept these old glasses tucked away in a utility drawer for so long?

Melanie never knew her grandmother very well. Grandpa Lane died when Melanie was small, and for as long as Melanie could remember after, Grandma had refused to leave her house. Melanie did recall the glasses, though, and how Grandma Lane would sit, humming, on her couch, her eyes focused somewhere else. Sometimes Grandma would talk to no one in particular; she'd giggle like a schoolgirl in love, or ask questions, alone in her living room.

"What would you like for dinner?"

"Did you check on the baby?"

"We're out of milk, dear. Would you go to the market today?"

When Melanie or Amanda would answer her, their response was met with soft humming. It was as if their grandmother didn't see them through those thick and glittery glasses, as if they weren't there in that room with her.

Mom and Dad said Grandma Lane had a sickness, which Melanie perceived years later as some sort of cognitive impairment, even dementia. And though they were told to be good and quiet while in Grandma's house, the backs of their hands were never reliable enough to stifle their giggles as they watched the old woman waltz around a room devoid of music, alone. When Grandma Lane was lucid and could hold a conversation, she'd told them about how the souls of the dead would find themselves stuck in the limbs of mighty oak trees if they didn't live a good and virtuous life. She told them that sand sharks lived on the moon and it was their daily migration that led to its waxing and waning. And that the glittering gold eyeglass case would bite and devour the fingers of naughty children who dared ever touch it.

Yet there Melanie stood, case in hand, her fingers intact as she studied the picture.

"What was going on behind those eyes?" Melanie whispered, caressing the pearls and rhinestones–jeweled blemishes marring the frames' smoothness, yet defining its character. A bit like Grandma Lane herself.

I wonder what I'd look like in these glasses, Melanie thought. She'd already committed the ultimate sin of childhood by touching the case. With no one to chastise her, why not try them on?

Screws loose, the frames offered little resistance as she opened them. Still staring at Grandma Lane's photo, Melanie lifted the glasses to her eyes.

The room blurred beneath the thick lenses. Then, everything changed.

***

The aroma of tomato and garlic tickled Melanie's senses, the air thick, laden with the steam from boiling water and meatballs simmering in sauce. A tap-tap-tapping–*Mom's wooden spoon*—against a pot. The tinny announcer and roaring cheers from the television inside the living room–*Giants game?* Both blew away the kitchen's silence, swift as the wind on an autumn day.

It was time for Sunday dinner.

But how?

Melanie grabbed the handle of the refrigerator and turned

toward the stove. Mom stood, stirring an oversized pot, her blue 'weekend' sweatshirt splattered with tiny drops of sauce. Her permed blond hair frizzed over her scalp, touches of gray teasing her temples with hints of age either unrecognized or ignored.

"Mom?"

Melanie squeezed the handle. Her eyes watered under Grandma Lane's glasses. Her face flushed. The kitchen lights pulsed, at once dimming and brightening like a maddening strobe in slow motion. Her head throbbed.

"Mom?"

"The fridge isn't going to open itself, Mel-Belle."

Mel-Belle. No one called her Mel-Belle except for Mom.

Mom placed her left hand on her hip, stirring with her right. *Just like I do*, Melanie thought.

"The cheese?"

"Oh, right. The cheese."

Melanie opened the refrigerator. Filled and organized, just as Mom liked it. Meats to the left, dairy to the right. And jugs of Melanie's favorite Hi-C fruit punch, like a demarcation line through the middle.

Melanie lifted Grandma Lane's glasses up from her eyes to her forehead.

Silence

The soundlessness sucked life from the room.

Stale air grabbed Melanie by the throat, leaving her gasping.

Three lonely bottles of water stood sentinel in the bare refrigerator.

Melanie dropped the glasses on to the bridge of her nose. She stared hard through the lenses and the soundtrack of her family's life resumed, like a warped record finding its track.

"Melanie, the cheese!"

She jumped at her mother's voice and grabbed the half-filled plastic container from the bottom right shelf, smiling at the *La Famiglia* logo emblazoned on the lid. They always made the best fresh ravioli. In the years since it had closed, it had transitioned to a deli (Nick's), a card shop (Solo's), and most recently, a nail salon (Eden's).

"Here you go...Mom," Melanie's voice croaked. She looked upon her mother's face, smooth and rounded as she remembered it from her childhood. The corners of Mom's lips curled upward, as if she'd swallowed a secret.

My mother, here again, Melanie thought. Not that shadow of a woman hunched over a cane in those final months, shuffling down an antiseptic hospital hallway for another chemotherapy session. Not that gaunt woman hiding a bald head beneath a winter cap in the middle of summer. Not that tiny, shriveled someone who slipped away in the quiet of hospice, her hands as cold as the dawning winter.

My mother, living and real and vibrant.

Just as Melanie remembered her. As she wanted to remember her.

"You feel okay, Mel-Belle?" Mom leaned over and kissed Melanie's forehead, her double chin grazing the top of the glasses. "You look a little peaked."

"I'm... I'm fine," Melanie said. Mom tugged the cheese canister away from Melanie's grip. She opened the lid, sprinkling the cheese into the pot as she stirred.

"Ready for the Spelling Bee finals tomorrow?" Mom asked.

The spelling bee. Seventh grade. Knocked out of the state competition by the word 'percolator.' She'd blamed her mother's New York accent for the gaffe—there was no 'u' in percolator, no matter how Mom pronounced it.

"Spell omelet," Mom said.

"Mom!"

"Omelet. Come on. You can do this. I have faith!"

The memory flitted at the edge of Melanie's mind, fleeting, like a butterfly's kiss.

"O-M-L-E-T-T-E."

Mom scowled. "Did you study? Did you *really* study?"

"I... I did study."

"Study harder. You need to work at this if you want to move on." Mom shooed Melanie away with a waving palm. "Go tell your father it's almost time to eat. And stop playing with those old glasses. You're going to give yourself a headache."

"A headache," Melanie murmured. Her chest seized her breath before she could exhale again, before this moment would dissipate, like so many other mundane, yet remarkable moments that hover like dust motes, floating and immobile despite the whirlwind of life. Staring at her mother, Melanie took in every detail. There were so many things she'd forgotten, overlooked in the day to day, perhaps—the beauty mark under her mother's left eye, the way her earlobes drooped beneath her heavy earrings. Melanie leaned into her mother, wrapping her arms around her soft, ample midsection. She laid her head on her mother's chest. Mom's heartbeat thrummed into Melanie's temple like a forgotten lullaby.

"I love you, Mom," she whispered.

"I love you, too," Mom said, rubbing Melanie's back. "Now, go get Daddy for me while it's still halftime, otherwise we'll lose him to football forever."

Melanie nodded, extricating herself from her mother. She shivered as she walked toward the living room on wobbly legs, as much from the loss of Mom's warmth as from the anticipation of seeing her father.

"Dad?" Melanie called. She stepped into the living room, her feet—Melanie noticed, clad in her favorite 80s jelly shoes and wigwam socks—sunk into the beige shag carpet. Her father snored on the old blue couch, his mouth open, beer belly jiggling with each breath. She smiled, knowing that if she woke him, he would deny having been asleep. *Just resting my eyes*, he used to say.

Seeing Dad again was like finding a rainbow on a sunny day. He'd had a much more peaceful death than Mom. She'd slipped beneath the murky depths alone, hands too weak from fighting to grab hold of any lifeline tossed out to her. Whereas Dad, he left in his sleep, healthy except for the heart attack that claimed him. Melanie always envisioned her father waving to the family as they saw him off from the shoreline—a final bon voyage as he rowed into calm waters on his own terms, his death resolute and absent the struggle her mother endured in her battle with cancer. And now, lush, thick grass filled Dad's burial plot, while the earth was still so fresh on Mom's grave–unsettled and raw. *Funny how time's sleight-of-hand seals away the pain of loss,* Melanie thought. So preoccupied with the loss of her mother, she had forgotten how much she missed her father.

The fall breeze lifted the sheer curtains, grazing the bronze lamps on the end table with a spectral touch. Melanie glanced at the framed photographs on the wall; her own eyes stared back at her with the wide-eyed questioning of infancy, the shyness of toddlerhood, the seriousness of school age. Always heavy, tentative, Melanie thought. Unlike Amanda, whose portraits seemed to float from the walls with a smiling confidence.

Melanie raised the glasses up over her eyebrows. Again, the walls loomed in their dusty nakedness–artifacts of childhood vanished with a glance. The sharp silence lurched her into the focus of now. Was it hours, days, or decades since Melanie had cursed her sister for leaving her alone in the house? She neither remembered, nor cared.

As she repositioned the glasses on the bridge of her nose, the TV glowed, crowd roaring to another Giants touchdown. Dad's snoring boomed in the cacophony.

"Dad." Melanie sat on the couch and touched his shoulder, shaking him. "Dad."

He jolted awake. "Oh! Hi, honey. I was just resting my eyes."

Melanie smiled. "I know, Daddy."

He yawned, stretching. "What's the score?"

"28 to 3. They're crushing the Redskins."

"Ah, that's my Big Blue. Halftime's over?"

"Over."

He pushed himself up and ruffled Melanie's hair as he stood. "Something smells good. Mom's making meatballs?"

"Wouldn't be a Sunday if she didn't."

It wouldn't be a Sunday if she didn't. Melanie wondered how many meatballs her mother had cooked over the years. How many times they'd sat around that table, laughing or fighting or complaining. What little things were so funny, so annoying, or important? Had she ever realized that the last Sunday dinner they'd shared would be *the* last? Had she known, would she have done anything different? Would she have lingered at the table longer, or laughed louder at her father's jokes?

Melanie stood and squeezed her father's hand. Eyebrow raised, he glanced at her.

"Daddy? Can I ask you a question?"

He nodded.

"If you had to leave this house today and you could never come back, what's the one thing you'd take with you?"

Dad scrunched up his lips and scratched the back of his hand. His thinking pose.

"Can I take the television? To watch my Giants?"

She fought the urge to roll her eyes. "No, I mean something important."

"Well, that's easy," he said. "I'd take my family. You, Mom, and Amanda."

"Needs to be a thing, not a person."

"Nothing."

"Nothing?" Her father rarely offered anyone a straight answer, but when he did, his words somehow always blew through the fog.

"Nothing. No thing." He tapped his chest. "I have what I need right here. For as long as I live."

Melanie swallowed hard, wriggling her nose in warning to the tears that prickled the corners of her eyes.

"But what about... after?"

Dad pulled Melanie in for a hug. The glasses jostled against her face as Dad gave her a hard kiss on the forehead.

"After? Do you know something I don't?"

Melanie opened her mouth and promptly closed it, unsure of how to respond. Dad chuckled.

"I'll tell you what. I'll come back someday and let you know."

Melanie heard her mother tap the wooden spoon against the sauce pot three times. "Dinner!" Mom yelled.

"Better go get your sister," Dad said. "You know Mom hates it when she lollygags to the dinner table."

Dad turned and walked into the kitchen. Melanie watched as he rested his hand on Mom's back and she turned to kiss his cheek. The smallest gesture writ the volume of decades, their connection severed only by death. But perhaps not.

A poster of an 80s teenage heartthrob greeted Melanie as she approached Amanda's room. She knocked once and opened the door. "I told you to stay out!" Amanda shrieked through the asynchronous beat of some pop song playing on her oversized stereo. Melanie was bowled over by the shrill electronic synthesizer and the whining vocals that dug into her eardrums like a ravenous worm and by the shoe Amanda flung at her, hitting her between the eyes.

Cracking Grandma Lane's glasses in half.

The eye pieces melted from Melanie's face as if in a Dali painting. Melanie caught the remnants in her palms before crumbling to the floor in the re-birthed silence.

"No," she whispered, squeezing tight fists around the plastic. The rhinestones dug into her skin as the pearls soothed. Melanie brought her hands together, imploring whatever mystic force that enchanted the glasses to repair the broken pieces she held—to fix the broken pieces inside her. Releasing her grip, Melanie stared at the remnants resting in her palms.

She lifted the lenses up, one in each hand, and placed them in front of her eyes. She fought the strain pulling at her eyes as she squinted through the lenses. What was clear before became nothing more than a migraine-inducing haze. The harder she looked, the more it hurt. Stiff tears clouded her view, thick as cataracts.

Melanie wanted her mother back. She wanted to sit at that table, one last time, and tell her mother everything—or tell her nothing at all. She wanted to sit with her Dad as he watched the end of the game, legs tucked beneath her on the corner of the couch, the drone of crowds and announcers the auditory backdrop of a lazy Sunday afternoon.

I'm an orphan, Melanie thought. *A 43-year-old orphan.*

She yearned to live in that world she saw through Grandma Lane's glasses. The world where her parents lived and breathed and thrived; where the tang of Sunday pasta dinners lingered ever-sweet on her tongue and home swaddled her with the softness of a worn blanket left at her bedside on a cold night.

Her lower lip quivered; her shoulders shuddered.

She didn't attempt to stop the tears. The dam she'd built with the detritus of grief and regret ruptured, unleashing a tsunami of feelings she'd avoided for so long. After her parents' death, the house had become nothing but a cold, empty shell that Melanie feared would swallow her whole. Yet with those glasses, she saw things she'd always taken for granted, wrapped in the warmth of smells and sound and light and laughter that painted her home. Her story. She tasted the salt of pent-up bitterness, the sweet nectar of release, and remembered what was good.

Yet, the image of her grandmother, twirling alone in her living room, danced across Melanie's memory. For the first time, Melanie realized it wasn't dementia that trapped Grandma Lane within her own mind; the sickness afflicting her was an unrelenting longing for the past.

As beautiful as that past was, Melanie wouldn't spend her life hiding. It was time to move forward. Time to move on. Melanie laughed through her sobs.

"You ok in there, sis?" Amanda burst through the front door, slamming it behind her. "I know, I'm late. I'm sorry." Melanie looked up to see her 47-year-old sister in wrinkled work-out clothes, graying hair falling from her messy bun. Crows' feet punctuated years in the corners of her eyes.

"The kids were driving me crazy today. One crisis after another."

Melanie threw herself into Amanda's arms, squeezing her hard.

"Oof," Amanda said, pulling away. "I'm surprised you're here. I thought you would have bailed hours ago."

"I'm glad I didn't." Melanie smiled. "I did some hard work today."

"I knew you could," Amanda said. "And you did it, alone."

I wasn't alone, Melanie thought.

"Thanks, Sis," she said. "For everything."

Melanie pocketed the pieces of Grandma Lane's glasses and linked her arm through her sister's. Together they walked through the skeleton of their childhood home. Melanie felt an odd peace in the bare walls and empty rooms that hours before brought only pain. Melanie finally saw beyond her grief, grateful to find that one tile in the mosaic that maintained its beauty, despite the fissures that marred the others around it.

Melanie had found an unexpected treasure in the chaos of that junk drawer. Had her mother known of its magic? Or was it simply a relic tucked away, out of sight and mind, though ever present and comforting?

Something like our best memories.

The important things, Melanie would always carry them inside. No matter where she went, she knew she'd always be home.

Small Offerings for a Small God

Virginia M Mohlere

Virginia M. Mohlere was born on one
solstice, and her sister was born on the
other. Her chronic writing disorder
stems from early childhood. She lives
in the swamps of Houston and writes
with a fountain pen that is extinct in the
wild. Her work has been seen in Cicada,
Lakeside Circus, Journal of Unlikely
Coulrophobia, Strange Horizons, and
Mythic Delirium, among others. This
story is for tumblr user iguanamouth.

"You will worship me."

Danit's armor paused, a rarity; she raised her eyes from the sand immediately in front of her feet to the shape before her.

The godling was little more than a vaguely cylindrical cloud with snapping black eyes at approximately the height of her collarbones.

"Or what?" Danit said.

It wasn't as if being *more* cursed would make much of a difference.

"You will worship me," the godling repeated.

"If you like," she said. "But I'll have to do so at a walk."

The armor moved; she moved with it.

Danit didn't know whether the godling followed her until the sun set and she was allowed to stop. But when she finished gathering her bits of wood for the evening and sat, a misty shape bunched up on the ground across from her.

Determined little thing. Danit set aside one of the kindling-sized sticks; once the fire was crackling, she waved it in the godling's direction, kissed it, and stuck it upright in the flames, where it would burn vertically. The mist convulsed, as if the godling shuddered. Danit closed her eyes to take advantage of not having to walk in the dark.

In the morning, the godling was a little more substantial—still blurry, but bipedal, with dark hair to match its eyes. Danit's canteen and the pack around her waist were filled, as they were each morning. She flicked a few drops of water onto the sand in the direction of the godling as the low-angled sun hit her legs and they moved. Throughout the day's light-enforced trudge, Danit dropped shreds of walking rations on the ground, shook wet fingers when she drank, in case she was still followed.

The godling again sat across her fire that evening, closed dark eyes when she dedicated another stick to them. Was she allowed to feel satisfaction anymore? Regardless, she did, and no new aches were added to her catalog in response to her gladness that her small gestures fed this pet godling she'd acquired.

"I can pray, if you like," Danit said. "What's your name?"

The godling's black eyes seemed to take up a greater proportion of the blob that made up their face.

"I don't know," they said. "It's been too long."

Danit shivered. Was that to be her fate, too, to walk until she lost even her name? Already the war seemed vague, and she had whole afternoons of wondering why she'd been so afraid of the axe.

"What are you the god of, then?"

"I don't remember."

The godling disappeared along with their rasp of misery. Danit lay down and let the thing that passed for sleep pull her in until the sun rose again, she walked again.

Curious that two silent days were enough to make her feel lonely at the godling's absence. Her walk's silence was heavier than before.

Wind and time had erased her tracks, but this section of scrubland seemed familiar. At least twice so far she had turned around to walk back across the waste. If she survived long enough, would she know every rock and scraggly tree?

She lit her offering for the godling, despite the empty space on the other side of her fire.

When the sun rose, and Danit's armor with it, he stood next to her. More solid, still small in stature but angular and beautiful. Frowning under heavy, arched eyebrows.

Maybe he would smite her and end this walking business.

Her armor moved. She couldn't feel much from the neck down, not even the filth she must be covered in under the plate mail. But she knew that the gorget rested differently on her shoulders recently, as if it were too big. She knew that the unconsciousness she found at night wasn't the rest of sleep, that the pain of sun and fatigue lanced through her head at the level of her right eye. She would walk herself to death, as ordered. Her armor might even continue to walk afterward. She would never know.

"You made offerings even when you couldn't see me," the god said. "Why?"

"Why not?" Danit said. "There isn't much I'm allowed, but if that gesture helps, I can think of no reason not to make it."

"Offerings made in faith have more power," the god said. "My form has mass, now."

"Good," Danit said.

He didn't speak again that day, though he drifted around her in circles, frowning as he watched her stare at his face and her body skirted a scrubby tree without her looking. Perhaps time moved differently for gods: he stayed silent while she made her small offerings to him, all the way through to the next night.

She was approaching the edge of the waste: bushes clumped around more-substantial trees at regular intervals. Soon the armor would turn, and she'd walk across the waste again. For the—fourth? fifth? time.

"What is the curse on you?" the god asked from across her fire.

"To walk," Danit said. "The armor walks while sunlight hits it, and I walk within it."

"It kills you."

"Yes."

The god crept close, peered at her. He smelled like ozone. She could see lights inside the darkness of his eyes. Danit felt vaguely nauseated, staring into the eyes of a god.

The god tugged at the edge a plate, then snatched his hand back, hissing.

"This is a mighty curse," he said. "Why do you bear it?"

"I fought on the wrong side of a war," Danit said.

"This is the will of your conquerors? Did they treat all their defeated so?"

Danit shook her head.

"Not all. Just those of us in charge. We were, as I say, on the wrong side."

The god sat back on his heels. With more distance between them, his eyes no longer made Danit feel sick.

"You speak an obscuring truth," he said.

What were gods for, if not confession before death? Even if her death might take another month or three.

"I was a Field Marshall in the army of the Hassetic Empire. After twenty years enslaving the entire continent, a number of the population grew tired of us."

The godling tilted his head.

"Obscuring again."

"Well, you know, my sins are severe and many," Danit said. "It's not as if I enjoy speaking of them."

"Then why commit them?"

The armor would let her sit by the fire, tend it, eventually lie down. It did not permit her to shrug.

"To hold the lives of the weak in my hands was a heady power," she said, though it hurt her throat to do so. "To make those lives suffer and end on my whim was more alluring still."

The godling stood; lightning flashed around his dark eyes.

"It has been two ages of civilization since I was last worshipped," he spat. "And you are corrupt of heart."

He disappeared with the sound of distant thunder.

Five days, he left her alone. Danit reached the edge of the waste Her armor turned for the trudge back across. Each time before, she had been alone. This was the first time that the turning rang hollow in her chest and she felt the weight of her armor shift around her.

She still lit offerings for the godling, still flicked water onto the ground. She sat by her evening fire while silence crowded her. She lay with her eyes open and watched the stars march across the sky as she marched across the waste, then stood inside her armor at dawn, head throbbing in time with her heart and eyes sandy, to walk alone.

On the fifth night, the silence was a horror that choked her, and Danit prayed.

When she had held lives in her hands and spent them like straw cast to the ground, she had felt herself equal to the gods, made her sacrifices with an empty heart. Now she prayed to a tiny god whose name she didn't even know with a voice scratchy with disuse.

Danit didn't mean to be sorry. She hadn't thought she was sorry, just afraid of the axe, and the blood that fountained from the necks of the other officers, her Empress. She had strode the battlefields of a continent, victorious and powerful—she wasn't supposed to be afraid to wink out and become nothing.

But she was. She had chosen this curse, to walk the waste in this armor, winding down like unattended clockwork, until she winked out after all, shriveled and filthy, instead of all at once in a river of blood. She cursed the godling for making her examine herself when she could've continued to walk without thought until she ended.

She sat by her fire and wept onto the ground for the godling who came to her unbidden, granted her the blessing of a chance to perform one generous act, and took himself away again.

"Forgive me," she said to the stick burning vertically among the flames. "You deserve a better worshipper."

"I accept your penance," the godling said.

Danit stared at the feet just within her vision, finely shaped and clean of all the sand that surrounded them. She looked up, and the light of the fire bent away from his face, so that his eyes were shadow inside shadow, lit only by flickers of lightning.

"You are weak, Danit Ellinsdottir," he said.

"I am."

She was glad that he was now strong enough to pull her name out of her head.

The godling crouched, arms around his knees. Maybe Field Marshall Danit Ellinsdottir, conqueror of nations and holder of ten thousand lives, would've presumed to read the expression of a god. Danit of the waste kept her eyes on his left cheekbone, tried not to mind the tickle of her dripping nose and tears drying on her cheeks.

"What you do not see is that your weakness makes an opening in your curse," the godling said.

Danit tried to remember a time when anyone had ever spoken to her with such tenderness. She failed. She looked into the godling's lightning-lit eyes.

"I could touch your armor now and take it from you," he said.

She could stop walking. Her body would be her own again. The body she hadn't felt since the curse spelled her armor to move.

"Will I live?" she asked.

His eyes flickered.

"I do not know."

Was it living that she did, walking the waste? Or simply drawing out the fate that had waited for her since the moment of the empire's defeat?

"Is there redemption?"

Lightning crackled around the godling's face, but the set of his mouth wasn't unkind.

"I am no death god," he said. "The human afterlife is unknown to me. But your worship has given me form and mass when I had none, so the blessing of this small god will go with you, whether you live or no."

"Take it," Danit said from the raw place deep inside her chest.

The godling touched her cuirass. The armor fell away from her, releasing all the sensation it had hidden: pain, itch, the scratch of weeping sores, and the scent of her own filth. A fatigue so profound that Danit fell sideways, unable to control her own withered, spent muscles.

The godling caught her, lowered her head onto his knees and smoothed the hair out of her face.

Even her eyelids felt too heavy to control. Darkness pulled, inexorable, and it wasn't even illuminated like the flicker of the godling's eyes.

"Your walk is over," he said. "Be done. Whether you wake or end, for your faith I will stay with you."

With the final drop of her stubbornness, Danit watched storms brew in her godling's eyes. She prayed once again, a final "please" with no idea what she asked for, lying on the lap of a small god.

She closed her eyes.

Sleeping Giants

Erin Keating

Erin Keating is a grant writer at an arts education nonprofit. She earned her B.A. in creative writing and literature at Roanoke College. Her fiction is forthcoming in METAPHOROSIS.

Annie Warren spoke in tongues—every time she opened her mouth garbled sound flooded out. The only people on God's green Earth who knew were her ma and pa. They told her never to speak in front of strangers, and the girl listened.

They told the neighbors she was mute. Better to have a mute girl than a girl who speaks in tongues. Lord knows what people might've done to her. There were God-fearing men in the valley and Mrs. Warren still remembered what happened to the old woman at the edge of town when whispers started floating that she was a witch. Her whole shanty burned to the ground in the middle of the night, the woman and her cats dying of smoke. No one would ever admit to the arson, of course. But everyone had their suspicions.

So it went that Annie Warren never spoke a word in public until the summer she turned nine. That was the same summer they put the railroad in. Looking back, she should have known what was going to happen, but at the time she had been too young to understand.

Annie woke one morning to the sound of squawking birds in panicked flight. She rushed to the window and watched them fly from their trees as a metallic ringing pierced the valley. Annie had never heard the sounds of war before, but she imagined that was what it sounded like. Before she could let out a cry, her pa appeared beside her and scooped her up on his back.

"Now lil' miss. Don't you worry about nothing." He bounced her once on his back until she giggled. "They're just laying down ties. And your pa is gonna help them. Let's you and I walk down there together."

Annie always walked barefoot. She tried to explain why to Ma and Pa once, though they couldn't understand her. She hadn't minded. They tried their best, Annie knew. But they didn't know how to listen.

Annie listened to everything. She listened through her feet, through her hands. As she walked alongside her pa, pressing her calloused heels into the dusty road, she listened. Above the line of trees she saw great black clouds as though the forest was burning. She expected to hear the crack and hiss of blistering wood, but the earth was silent. There were no cries of agony from the branches. Only muffled splutters from the gray sky. No, the forest was not burning. It was choking.

She wanted to ask her pa why they were walking towards that black cloud. But she knew better than to speak in public. Her family had taught her that silence would keep her safe. Instead, she clutched her pa's hand and whimpered.

"Don't you worry lil' miss." He grinned at her with a snaggle-tooth smile. She smiled back, but she could not relieve the sickness in her stomach.

Annie wanted to shout, "Can't you hear anything?" but she knew the words would warp on her tongue.

So Annie walked silently with her pa, pulling at the hem of her dress, as the earth gasped for air. The earth knew that she could understand it, and every tree she passed seemed to rustle its branches at her in disdain. They accused her: how dare she not do anything?

Annie had helped before, in her small ways. When the flowers were dying in the cold, she huddled beside them, speaking rays of sunshine from her mouth. When the crops were dying in the drought, she lay in the dirt, under the moon, letting rivers flow from her words. Annie could make things *be*. And all she needed was her words.

When her pa stopped at the edge of a clearing, the banging and clanging had become so loud Annie felt as though nails were being hammered through her heart. She did not try to look at her pa for reassurance anymore and, instead, balled the hem of her skirt tighter in her fist. Her pa would tell her not to worry. His words would be useless.

From the clearing, Annie could peer in the valley below. Through the clouds of coal dust and dirt she could see men hammering away, slamming spikes into railroad sleepers. They were laying down tracks, just like her pa had said. Carts were pushed back and forth on the tracks, a horrible clattering noise that echoed off the mountains. The railroad stretched like a long scar through the valley. Something once perfect no longer was.

Annie looked up at the storm clouds sweeping in over the mountains. Everyone thought they were nestled away so safely in their valley, but Annie knew the truth. Her little village rested in the palm of a sleeping giant. A gray thunder cloud hovered over the giant's shoulder for a moment before racing across the sky. The earth rumbled, sending fresh panic through Annie's little body. The earth had told her a lot of things, but she had never felt anything quite like this before. The giant was stirring.

"You run back to Ma, okay? I'm gonna spend me some time with these fellers. They say the pay is good. You'll run and fetch me when it's time for supper?" Pa asked.

Annie nodded, but she wanted to scream.

***

So it went for some time. Annie got up in the mornings with Pa and walked down to the new railroad. She would wave to him from the edge of the trees before running home to help Ma in the garden. It never rained during that time Annie's pa worked on the tracks. It only thundered. All the while, every night before she went to sleep she heard the sounds of the earth gasping for air.

Annie went out into the garden one night, when the earth's choking kept her awake. In the darkness, she couldn't see the black cloud that hung over the railroad tracks. She wondered if it was still there or if it had settled into dust. Digging her fingers into the soil, she felt the earth shake with fear. No, the black cloud was still there, and the giant was still angry.

She sat down in the garden, her dark hair disappearing under the rows of corn stalks. Under her voice, for fear of waking up the neighbors, she sang to the winds. Annie wasn't sure what the song would have sounded like to those passing by, but there, alone in the darkness, she thought her melody was beautiful.

Gooseflesh rippled across her skin as the first wind swooped down. It rustled her hair and rattled the corn stalks as it rushed over the garden. She imagined it flying over their town and through the trees at the edge of the tracks. What she would have given to watch that wind plow through that coal cloud, scattering it with one great poof. Her fingers still gripping the dirt, she heard the earth take its first real inhale. Annie exhaled.

The earth thanked Annie. Despite it being the middle of the night, Annie watched as a small green vine pushed upwards through the soil, unfolding into a bright blue morning glory. It was the same color as Annie's eyes. She whispered her thanks to the earth, plucked the flower, and tucked it behind her ear.

Annie slept soundly that night. She thought the railroad couldn't do any more harm now.

***

The next morning, when Annie walked down to the tracks with her pa, his lunch pail bumping against both of their legs, she felt the earth tug at her feet.

"It's alright," she wanted to tell it. If she could have spoken, she would have said, "Nothing can hurt you now."

But she remained silent. The earth tugged at her feet harder. Annie dragged her feet with each step she took.

"Are you alright, lil' miss?" Pa asked.

Annie looked at him with her wide blue eyes and nodded. She kicked dust up with her feet, telling the earth she would go to the tracks and that was final. Thunder growled overhead. Annie whispered an apology under her breath. The sky remained as gray as ever.

When Annie and Pa reached the clearing, he stopped and patted her head. "I love you lil' miss."

Annie knew he wouldn't understand her if she said it back.

***

Later that evening, Annie leaned against the window while her ma paced in front of the door. On the table, supper was getting cold. Annie longed for the honey biscuits, but she knew they wouldn't eat until Pa came home.

Ma leaned over Annie, looking out the window one last time. Annie always thought her ma was like a bird, flitting from one thing to the next. Ma took a few helpings of biscuits and a good chicken wing and wrapped it up nicely in a cloth. "He must be working late. Can you bring him his supper?"

Annie took the cloth in her hand and Ma kissed her on the head. "Come right back. And don't talk to anyone." Annie rolled her eyes at her ma. "I know, you know. Now go." She patted Annie's backside and scooted her out the door.

Annie ran down the dusty road, listening to the earth hollering at her as she went. With each step it tried to slow her, tugging at her feet, reaching up to grab her ankles. She kicked and stomped as she rushed along, tripping over the earth that struggled to hold her still. "I have to give food to Pa," she whispered under her breath. The road was empty. There would be no one around to hear her. "Why won't you let me go?"

Lightning flashed in the sky, just over the railroad tracks. The cloth of food slipped from her fingers. She understood.

The earth did not try to slow her now. She tore down the road and through the woods. Around her, the trees whispered con-dolences. Branches reached out to touch her shoulders, offering comfort. Annie paid them no mind. She brushed them off and kept racing ahead, until she stood at the top of the clearing, look-ing down into the valley.

A cluster of men stood around a broken body. From her spot on the hill, she couldn't see the face of the dead man, but she knew at once who it was.

"Pa!" she cried. It was no longer his name when it left her lips, but the warped cry of a wounded animal. The rail workers in the valley turned to look up at her.

She ran down the hill, fell, and got back up to keep running. When she reached the circle of men, they wouldn't let her through. She was stopped by a wall of arms; hands pulled at her shoulders and hair. Their voices told her "get back, don't look".

She gnashed her teeth at them and wailed. The earth understood her sorrow. For the first time in weeks, the thunder clouds opened up, and it began to rain.

"Come on, kid." One of the men squatted down to Annie's height. The rain washed streaks through the dirt on his face. He held her arm. She hated the way his calloused touch felt on her skin. "You should go home. He's not coming back."

She tried to wrestle out of his grip and get closer to Pa, but the man only held on tighter.

"Let her look," one of the men said quietly. He had a wide hat that covered his eyes. Water dripped from its brim.

"Come on, we should clean him up first. She shouldn't have to see that." The man holding Annie's arm let go of his grasp.

"Do you want to see your daddy?" the man with the hat asked. Annie nodded. He took off his hat and held it in front of him. He gestured to the men and they stepped to the side, opening like a gate to her pa. Annie looked up at their faces as she walked by them—all of the grown men looked at her with pity.

Annie knelt in the grass next to her pa, trying to find a memory of him inside that broken body. The arms that used to carry her were bent at unnatural angles. His usually smiling face still registered the surprise of the runaway cart. No one had bothered to close his eyes—blue like hers. She almost reached out to touch him, but was afraid she would break him even more. The rain sent the dried blood at Pa's crown down his still face in rivers.

The earth was crying; the raindrops soaked through Annie's dress and turned the ground beneath her to mud. Annie wished she could cry. But the tears wouldn't come. Digging her fingers deep into the mud, she let out a scream. Annie felt something deep inside her break loose. Her face began to turn red. Her breathing came in short gasps. This was the kind of anger she had only ever seen, but never felt. This was the anger of the winds that could uproot trees. This was the anger of the waterfall beating away at rocks.

Suddenly, there was the sizzle of water striking heat. Annie looked down at her arm, so hot that each raindrop simmered against her skin and turned to steam. This was the anger of the sun.

She put her hand on the rails. They began to melt and the smell of steel crept into her nose. Annie clenched her teeth together and held onto a wooden railroad tie. With a yell, she pulled the tie out of the ground. The steel attached to it rippled like a wave. The tie crackled like wood on a fire. Annie stomped her foot and the world rumbled in support. It wasn't thunder. Annie knew better this time—it was the giant of the valley.

"How –?" the man with the hat began to ask. Annie couldn't hear the rest of his question over the shouts of the other railroad workers. They ran at her. Annie felt their hands—all of those hands—tugging at her dress and her hair.

For the first time in her life, Annie cursed. She brought hatred into being. The earth felt her pain and reached up, wrapping itself around the feet of the men. They kicked and cried as their legs became encased in mud. Annie did not yield. She continued her torrent of words, the curses warped on her tongue to something even more malicious. Wisteria vines crept out of the forest and slid down the hill. They wrapped themselves around the men's arms and pulled them to the ground. The men thrashed about, sending purple wisteria petals into the air.

The wind told Annie to run. She listened and didn't look back. She already knew what she would see: the men wrestling the wisteria and Pa's lifeless body on the tracks. Nothing she did would ever bring him back.

***

Annie ran home surrounded by a cloud of steam. The sky crackled with anger.

Ma was in the doorway, shouting, "Annie, get out of the storm!"

Annie let out a cry of relief upon seeing her ma. The mud squelched between her toes as she ran. She was soaking wet, covered in mud and blood, but her ma held her arms out to her.

"Annie, what happened?" she asked.

Annie ran into her ma's open arms. Ma screamed. She pushed Annie off of her. Bright red burns rose on her forearms and hands.

"What did you do?" Ma cried. Her skin began to blister.

Annie gestured to the rain. The rain would heal Ma. The earth would help. Ma wouldn't move. She just wept, holding her arms out in front of her.

"The rain! The water!" Annie shouted, pointing and jumping, but Ma wasn't listening.

"Please..." Ma whispered. "Please don't touch me." Ma backed into the house, while Annie stood out in the rain. The door swung between them.

The tears that Annie had longed for at the tracks began to sting her eyes. Pa was gone, and Ma... Ma was afraid of her. For the first time in her life, Annie felt like a monster. She curled up in front of the door, crying and screaming like the storm around her. The sweet smell of burning pine wood choked her and stung her eyes.

Annie scrambled away through the mud. There was a scorch mark on the door where her head had rested. She was a monster. A demon. A child of fire—destructive and uncontrollable. She cried, and kicked at the mud. She was alone.

A thought blew over her, calming her like a lavender breeze. It was up to the giant now, Annie thought. He had been stirring, and she would wake him. He would tear up the railroad. He would heal Ma. He would make sure no one was hurt like Pa again.

Annie wiped the tears from her eyes and pressed her hand against the door, leaving an imprint burned into the wood. It was a promise to Ma. Annie only hoped she would understand.

***

On the other side of the valley, the woods thickened. Spruce firs grasped the edge of the mountains. Annie held on to each trunk, pulling herself up the steep incline. The fir needles stabbed at her feet, but she couldn't feel anything anymore. When she lifted her hand from the tree bark, she left scorch marks behind.

She heard the sound of rushing water. Despite the roar of the rain around her, the earth whispered to her and she followed. Her feet burned the decaying leaves beneath her feet.

Annie found the river that had called her. It asked her softly, "Please?" Annie did not wait. Jumping into the water, she disappeared below the surface with a puff of steam. She screamed and let the bubbles fly from her mouth. Annie thought of Pa on the tracks. She wondered if Ma would ever find out what happened to him—or if she would ever see Ma again. The river held her as she cried, promising her it would be alright.

When Annie surfaced, it had stopped raining. She was no longer burning. Through the tops of the trees, she could see glimpses of the sun. She swam to the edge of the river and took a long, cool drink. Water dripping from her hair and dress, Annie continued her walk through the forest. This time, the earth did not fear her; instead, it reached out to help. Stones turned themselves into steps, letting her scale the side of the mountain. The earth whispered to her that she was not alone, and sang to her through the birds in the trees. Annie listened for Ma's call, but she never heard it. The earth was kind to her, but at that moment she longed to hear nothing more than her own name in her ma's mouth.

The line of trees began to thin, and then Annie broke right through them. She was at the summit, on the shoulder of the sleeping giant. Above her the sky was a mix of gray and blue, as the thunder storm continued to roll on. The smell of rain still hung in the air. Below her, in the valley, she could see the houses of her village, tiny brown flecks against the green fields. She tried to spot which house was hers, and wondered if Ma had treated her burns and begun to look for Pa. From this height, she couldn't see the railroad. The earth looked better that way.

She crossed the narrow ridge of the giant's neck, and climbed onto the pile of rocks she knew was his ear.

"Hello!" she shouted. "We need you!" The giant understood. The earth shook.

Experiment Ninety-Four

Sarah Salcedo

Sarah Salcedo is a writer, illustrator, and filmmaker based in the Pacific Northwest. Her writing has been published in Hobart After Dark, Not Deer Magazine, The Future Fire, Hypertext Magazine, and elsewhere. Her poetry has been featured at The Daily Drunk and in their Marvelous Verses anthology. Her first feature film documentary, Promised Land, won multiple awards. You can find her on Twitter at @SarahSalcedo or on her website, sarah-salcedo.com.

Originally published in *Collective Realms Magazine*, January 2021

The ship roared to life. Caspian was ready—to die or to escape, it was finally time to leave. Now or never. The centrifuge ring groaned into its rotation, lurching from the primary ring stasis lock. He could see the hammer strokes dappling the metal where he'd finished crafted them just a few months prior. As the ring picked up speed and began slicing through the thin atmosphere of the launch bay, artificial gravity hummed into his bones and shook his body.

He waited for the secondary ring to initiate. Fear burned in his chest. His fingers curled within his gloves to form fists, knuckles straining against the leather, haptic feedback buzzing in his palms. The ring rotations were howling. The *Evolo* had reached the center of the launch bay. *Any moment now.* He didn't know if what he had built was good enough.

Caspian tried to take a breath—possibly his last—as he released the mag tether keeping the ship bound to the station. *Destruction or escape.* The secondary rings were ready to engage.

He was ready for both.

***

In a decommissioned space station which orbited a nebula in a remote quadrant of space, there lived a boy named Caspian. He was alone, unloved, with nothing and no one but new stars to talk to as he spun through the darkness of space. He was a solution to a problem no one had asked him to solve, his loneliness a riddle with no answer.

His parents had abandoned him years before. They had forgotten him, lost him, or left him because there wasn't enough room in the escape pods—he didn't know. The station's defenses and artificial intelligence had been set to make sure he didn't starve to death or accidentally jettison himself out of an airlock. Caspian wasn't sure if their concern in these commands had been to protect him or the structural integrity of what had been their home. When he tried to remember his parents—to discern their intentions—a wave of nausea, a blurring of the room, consumed him with frightening intensity. Whenever he wept alone in his quarters, as any child would, the station's AI would put a stop to it. Prompting him with thin metal guides and gentle shocks to get up, go to lessons, get food, run on the track, Caspian learned not to cry. He learned to adapt. To survive.

Every morning, Caspian would wake up and race from his room to the track that ran along the circular main hallway. The ring-shaped station had an observation tower as its axis. It housed the station's power core. The craft resembled a bobbin threading a cosmic purple tangle in the nebula which it orbited. He used to run the circumference with his mother every morning before she left. She'd jog and he'd zigzag behind her, lost in games he would play.

"Run the path I'm running, Caspian," she would call back. He hadn't enjoyed listening to her back then, a regret that weighed his steps down years later as he ran the way she'd taught him.

The rotation of the station's outer ring created enough artificial gravity to create a stable environment that wouldn't distort human physiology. However, some of the *artgrav* regulators hadn't worked quite right in some areas of the station since the time of the evacuation. Caspian didn't mind the areas where gravity was weaker.

As he raced this path daily to the mess hall, he felt his body caught by the gravity in heavier sectors where the additional artgrav regulators were still functioning in harmony with the rotation of the station. He imagined he felt the pull of the station toward the nebula as it did its daily rotation, its axis tilting in degrees over the long 1,179 day circuit around the brumous birthplace for new stars. In the 2,976 days since he'd been left alone, he never grew tired of that feeling.

Nothing was wrong with the gravity in the mess. The droids in there were programmed to turn aminos into passable portrayals of what his father had called eggs scrambled. After getting food from the cookbot, Caspian settled on top of his usual table in the hall, right in front of the largest window in the station. He sat with his legs crossed, staring into the violet and scarlet heart of the nebula. Two glowing orbs within looked back at him boxed in by amber pillars jutting across the heart of the gas cloud, ethereal eyes observing the observation deck.

"Couldn't sleep last night," Caspian said. "Dreamt about them leaving again. The sirens. I almost remember—"

He shook his head and stared into a region of empty space, fixated on the black for a moment before looking back into the nebula.

The stars being birthed inside the nebula were more spotlights than actual stars: the collection of superheated gases were burning white, torches kindled in the night, as their gravity condensed the dust and gas around them. Caspian had started reading about their creation out of the ship's archives. He'd begun this out of boredom, but now made himself go through several hours of data every day. The ship's AI said his activities closely resembled the human tradition of "school."

The first thing Caspian had ever understood about his life was that the nebula was giving birth to stars, the way his mother would give birth to his baby brother. *They were observers*, they'd say. His parents had been there to study "the birth", as they'd called it, and he was there to learn about their work.

"New things take a long time to form," his father had said, patting Caspian's mother's stomach.

"The stars in this nebula will take up to 10 million years," his mother had replied. "They're just two bright eyes now."

"She'd be 54 today, you know," Caspian said to the nebula, shaking himself out of memories and back into the task of downing the *amineggs*. He had just over four minutes to finish them before they lost their shape and returned to a milky syrup.

"I wonder if she made it."

He looked at the pillars glowing in the darkness, hedging in the new stars. To him, they sometimes resembled a nose, or two of them, he supposed. The new stars were eyes as well as the nebula's children. *Lucky, to grow up with a sibling so close.*

"I might have a seven-year-old brother," he said to the nebula, tilting his head. The thought was unnerving. *If they'd lived, they would've had him five months later. Did he know he had an older brother?*

He slammed down his plate. He'd waited too long and the meal had deconstructed itself.

If they'd lived, they would've come looking for me by now.

He stormed out of the mess.

After breakfast, Caspian spent an hour in the gym. It had been his father's habit and he followed it, although it took him years to both grow into and figure out what the equipment was and how to use it without hurting himself.

Afterwards, he did school, then lunch, then more school, then dinner, then back to his room. His mother had brought hundreds of books from earth: volumes wrapped in leather, fabric, or rough paper with hundreds or thousands of pages each. He'd thought they were awkward to use when he was a kid, but in his teens, he was more eager to connect with anything they'd left behind.

When he'd panic, stories helped him breath deeper. Even the terrifying ones helped. No matter the plot, the construction of narratives—the idea that events, both good and bad, had meaning and that people, lost or found, successes or failures, were connected to each other by some larger journey—helped ease his mind.

After a few hours of reading, he'd ask the room to turn off the lights, increase the oxygen supply, and he'd drift off into what he always hoped would be a dreamless sleep. It rarely was.

***

"I'm not happy," Caspian said one morning. "Is that okay?"

The nebula did not answer.

"I don't think *you* can be happy," he continued, "but if you could, I'm sure you'd be happy about the state of things. After all," he gestured with a forkful of *amineggs* towards the nebula. "Your children are coming along nicely."

He imagined the nebula would be pleased to hear this.

"Coming along nicely," was his phrase for everything. Supply analysis projects, recalibrating and harvesting nebula dust from aerocombs, checking long-range sensors from the observation deck— whatever it was that his father did, if it avoided disaster, he would say it was "coming along nicely."

"I wonder if I can be happy," he paused to listen to the empty hum of the recirculated air through the ship, "if I stay here. Not that I have a choice in that. That's the worst part."

The twinkling furnaces shimmered copper and gold against the indigo gas around them.

"I know," Caspian's head dropped. "There's a pod left. But it's not steerable and it doesn't have anywhere near the thrust I'd need to leave. I'd just end up being pulled deeper into your gravity, joining you and the kids."

The nebula seemed to smile, a thin accretion of gold gas and dust arcing beneath the new stars. Some days it looked pessimistic. Today, it felt indulgent. Patient.

Not that being part of the new baby stars is unappealing. Caspian leaned on the window. *There are worse ways to go and any way to go may end up being better than this routine.* He thought of his mother's repetitive running through the circular hallways of the station.

"Follow my path," she'd call each morning. She was circling the nebula; he had been following her.

He frowned at the window, now focusing on the sharp image of his reflection against the vacuum of space.

The nebula dimmed as Caspian looked into his own eyes, dark as the void surrounding him.

***

It started small: agitation transmuting into a sharp determination.

Caspian began to dismantle things. He took apart equipment, monitors, and comm systems in unused parts of the station. He had no immediate reason other than wanting a kinesthetic knowledge of how things worked. He'd break something down, then he would build it again, studiously, before pulling it apart once more. When he finished, stripped parts went into component piles.

After a few years, his ability to disassemble an item — rather than destroy — was improving, as was his mechanical knowledge and ability to manipulate an object. Of course, he had other desperate motivations which he could not articulate yet.

He broke down chromatographs. Spectrographs. Micromanipulators. Temperature regulators. Months passed as the dismantling continued, until he came to the non-operational droids in storage. This was different. Cathartic. Caspian pulled each droid apart at the joint, breaking their limbs. He relished the tactile violence as he uncovered circuits, power sources, and wiring. Artificial ligaments popped, the casing snapped, data spines ripped from the top of automatons down along their frames.

After a day of this, his mind surfaced abruptly from the blur of his manual routine. His breath caught. In all his days of being served by the droids, he'd never actually touched one before this.

He hadn't touched anyone, mechanical or otherwise, in nine years. He looked down at the cybernetic arm he had been working on, a sudden feeling of loss and pain on behalf of the limb. He left the room without looking at the rest of the droids, both those already divided into supply piles and those waiting to be taken apart. It took days before he coaxed himself back to work. He didn't need servants; he needed parts.

After the droids, Caspian moved on to strip the station. There were living quarters around the station with a host of technologies: thermal, air, and gravitational regulators; biometric monitors; ship control interfaces and computers designed for the job of each member of the crew that had occupied them. He raided them, and then moved onto the gym, launch and storage bays, and broke down two of the three med bays. He rewired his educational lab to function as a smaller command center for the station before closing down the main command floor after he'd stripped most of its parts.

Some days, he was building a bomb—of sorts. A black hole engine would either get him to another outpost while he was still young or it'd kill him. It frightened him that he didn't care, that he would rather die than remain on the station where he was safe. Alone, but safe. Alone and without purpose. Or love. Or any definition of a life well-lived, as he'd read it in stories. But still—he was safe while he stayed. He didn't want to stay safe any longer.

On other days, when he wasn't tempting fate with black holes, he was designing a quantum vacuum engine he'd seen in files that the ship's chief engineer had kept. The science of both was barely within his grasp. He was bright and had never had anything better to do than learn from the lessons the station was programmed with or the logs left by the scientists and engineers who'd lived on the station. But being self-taught had its limits. Even if he could leave, he still hadn't solved the problem of turning a pod into a steerable craft with the resources he had on hand, and he took it out on any non-essential item he came into contact with.

Daily as he worked, the air felt tighter to him. It scraped through his throat, squeezed his wrists, bore down on his chest. Reading at night no longer reset his anxiety like it had—it goaded him on. None of his stories featured a character who was completely alone: they had friends, enemies, lovers, mentors. They had destinies and quests. Now, after reading, the ship felt smaller.

He checked in with atmospherics twice a day. Oxygen was normal. Temperature was normal. Gravity was the same as it had always been. But Caspian knew what he felt.

He was being compressed by the singularity of isolation. He didn't know how much longer he had until all hope of a sane life was lost.

***

It was the evening of his nineteenth birthday.

Caspian sat in silence in front of the nebula. He ate because he had to, taking the aminos in beverage or pill form. He had been doing this for years after he'd begun repurposing droids.

He looked up through the window and sighed, feeling his muscles relax a bit.

When everything had changed that morning, twelve years past, when he'd woken up to the loss of all he'd known, the nebula had been his only constant, the only connection to his parents, to the idea of a parent. The nebula gathered more than just cosmic material to her for the new stars—she gathered all his stories, all his imagination and longing for family and connection.

He smiled. She was always present, with her babies, celestial eggs woven within the nested striations of the gas cloud. Today, her thin gold mouth seemed skeptical.

Caspian's smile faded. He had been dreading telling her the truth about what he had been doing. She had never spoken before. *What would that voice even sound like?* But if she did or could speak, some small part of him feared it would be today.

"I'm leaving."

The nebula, as in the previous twelve years, said nothing in reply.

"I've figured out a few options, all risky. I'm not sure which one I'll choose." His pulse tripled; the air began to feel tight around his throat again. He saw disapproval reflected through the window.

"And if I do choose the bomb, it's not me giving up," he shouted. "There's only so much education programmed for me, besides obsessing over schematics I've found from other engineers. I can study all the data and crew backgrounds I want, but I can't make up for not knowing enough. It's not giving up if I can't make the thing work."

He hung his head.

"I know. Excuses."

He raised his chin again.

"It's just what my life has come to." He pushed away a tear with the palm of his hand and shook his head. "Joining you isn't the worst way to go."

He knelt by the window. This section of the nebula was more scarlet than violet, the amber portions of the nebula facing away from the station's current position.

His face was dark and crimson in the reflection. It was no longer a boy's face staring back. His image had a man's jaw line, a long crooked nose from when he'd broken it stripping parts last year, and dark hair. But his eyes were still those of the boy he had always been, looking out at the dual protostars incubating in the layers of gas and dust as if they were family, better known than his own.

He straightened up and backed away from the glass.

"We are watchers," his father had said once, when Caspian had asked to go visit the baby stars.

After he'd explained why the station was as close as it was possible to get to the stars without being crushed by their gravity, Father went on to explain the importance of research.

"Other people make things, but they don't get far without the facts that researchers provide them. Being able to watch without interference is an art, son. When you're old enough, you'll figure that out."

Caspian frowned at the memory. As he grew, he'd hoped some part of his features would grow to resemble his parents, or at least some part of his nature. But he was neither in form nor function like his family. He was made to act, not observe.

He couldn't wait any longer. He had to leave—no matter what came next.

***

The Experiment: Subject #94 has been isolated within the experiment for 4,801 days. The subject is showing signs of mental instability. My colleague insists the subject has formed a dissociative attachment to the "surrogate mother" that he's imagined of the nebula, I theorize that the subject's interaction with the nebula is a self-regulating mechanism, an anthropomorphization that the subject finds helpful but ultimately knows is fictional.

The subject's recent designs and early construction show he is either building a method of terminating himself or escaping the experiment.

This development will go a long way to prove his father's and my theories about the effects of long-term isolation for humans on deep-space colonization missions, especially on the efficacy of bred-explorers versus past programs' usage of adult conscripts who deteriorated after transitioning from colonies to deep-space missions.

If the subject is successful, the findings will have huge effects on the possibility of resuming the program's human-piloted expeditions to new habitable systems.

- Dr. Susan Thayer, 04.13.2117

***

The nearest settlement was a labor colony in the Wolf 1061 system, fifteen years away. If Caspian could reach it, he'd be thirty-six when he arrived.

He tried to stifle his anxiety at the thought. *It's still plenty of time.*

To get there, he needed at least thirty years of supplies. He trusted his navigational skills, but trusted his skepticism better. *A fool has one plan, but a wise man has three,* he'd read in one of Mother's old books once. He made sure to pack those as well. It was ambitious enough to design a deep space passenger vessel out of an oversized escape pod, but trying to design something to induce long-term hibernation was beyond him. The drugs that remained in the med bay would only help him manage anxiety. There was not nearly enough adenosine to induce the kind of state he'd need to sleep for more than a year. He needed every book, magazine, and game he could to preserve his mental state. He harvested these from his library as well as from abandoned crew rooms, unwilling to leave them despite the space they'd take up in his new ship. Books had provided him stability over the years.

Caspian rolled his eyes. He hoped they had.

Fifteen years of distraction to stave off madness. He shivered at the thought. He had been sorting supplies in the mess, one of the very few rooms he'd left intact. *I've only made it this far because I had room to run.*

His insides curdled as he pictured the tiny pod he was choosing over the vast space station. He looked up at the nebula and, for the first time, imagined what it would be like to see it from a distance. There were two portholes on either end of the craft. He'd be able to view the nebula as he traveled away from it. For a while, at least.

He blinked tears away. He would be losing family all over again. Caspian realized he'd stopped breathing. He tried to force down jagged breaths, picturing himself leaving in the tiny craft he'd retrofitted. The lights in the room seemed to grow dim. His whole body felt the splintered lack of oxygen, the tightening of each muscle.

He stared down at a mess of paper in his hands. In his panic, he'd ripped the spine of an ancient soft-back copy of Stephen King's *The Dark Tower*. He cringed and laid it gently down on the table beside him. He turned back to the nebula, twinkling back at him from the void.

"I don't know if I can do this."

***

Susan stares at Caspian from the Observation's vast monitoring deck. He is talking to the nebula again. Jack walks up next to her, an illuminated file hovering in front of him.

"Sensors show elevated cortisol levels." Jack looks up, an eyebrow raised. "Very elevated. Your side of the family."

"If he gets anything from either of us, he gets his analytical nature from me and his inability to handle stress from you. If he doesn't kill himself, it will be a testament to the way I raised him through the station."

"We designed this experiment, Susan. Together," Jack replies, once again focusing on the data. "I doubt he'll make it. The engine's use of the chameleon field is highly theoretical and there's no way to test it. Just the calculations of a child."

"That child is in his twenties and has been studying physics and engineering since he was eight. Not that it matters. If he doesn't make it, this experiment is still a success. He has become a team unto himself: engineer, mechanic, theoretician, captain, navigator..."

"If this team of one survives, then yes, it might support your theory that human explorers are once more superior to probes."

"Those raised in the program are," Susan snaps. "Probes are

limited. *They only discover what we tell them to, they don't ask, they don't—*"

"*Go insane? People do.*" Jack shakes his head.

"*Subject #94 has made it farther than the other subjects around the nebula. Only four of them have looked for a viable way off the station, and after #107's nuclear incident, #94 stands to make the first decent shot of it.*"

"*If he can escape the gravity of the nebula,*" Jack responds in a pedantic tone that makes Susan's back teeth hurt. "*Which he's not supposed to, I'll remind you. It's all well and good that he tries—that shows resilience—but this kind of thing is supposed to be beyond what they're able to do.*"

"*We're too far away to do anything about that.*"

"*You're only saying that because you're... attached.*" His lip curls in disgust at the word.

"*I'm saying that because I hope our experiment proves that humans can exist in deep space in isolation without going mad.*"

Jack shakes his head. "*He's one of hundreds, as is this particular experiment. One of them might prove your hypothesis. Many have proved mine.*"

They watch #94 storm out of the mess, several more torn books on the table.

"*I gave him* The Dark Tower *when he was six,*" Susan says. "*It was an accident—something silly and sentimental—but as I watch him talk to the nebula, I wish I'd done it with the others, to see how narratives help...*"

She trails off, realizing Jack has already walked away. She makes a *few notes before walking away herself to the next subject's screen. It bothers her, this aberration, caused by a moment of affection. Carelessness. It violates the control she needs.*

More experiments will have to be set up to replicate the results, test other variables, if he succeeds. Citizens always breed more than allowed by their colony's populace dispensation. Future subjects abound.

* * *

After another twenty months of work, Caspian's ship was ready to leave. He had installed communications systems and long-range sensors and waited until the station's orbit coincided with the best possible launch path for his course to the Wolf 1061 colony at Cepta Pactances. He had finalized the modifications to the Casimir thrusters and tested out the miniaturized version of the station's Sabatier life support generators for a month: tinkering with air quality, pressure, water, and waste before he was satisfied moving his books into the living compartment. He had two days and four hours to launch, according to his calculations.

He rolled his eyes at this. *According to my calculations.* He felt exposed by the amount of all he didn't know and wondered if his own mind was luring him into a trap.

Caspian tried to continue working. It was moving day and all his belongings were being sorted into their proper places. There was even a small treadmill he'd worked up. The centrifuge that he had outfitted around the craft to hold the engines would create a slight gravity bubble, roughly to the same degree that had enjoyed running on in the main hallway of the station. He hoped, as he installed it, that between it and the books, he wouldn't crack too early.

His breath became thin again, scratching against the shell of his chest.

I won't crack at all, he lied to himself. He knelt down and tried to force himself out of the rapid gasps. It'd been happening more often as he'd spent time working in the escape craft.

Caspian shook his head. He had to stop calling it that. He searched the compartment as if the name would be written somewhere obvious for him to read. All the names he knew were from stories, those left in the books from his mother or the crew. He wanted something that wasn't left behind, something that would remind him in the following years of why he was leaving home in the first place. He was searching for meaning by seeking others out. He was rejecting one home to find another. He clenched his fists.

"I *am* escaping," he said to his knees, holding them tight against his chest. "*Evolo.* I'm flying away."

He closed his eyes. It was a simple name. He felt it settle into him, exhaustion and relief releasing his muscles from the adrenaline. He got up and resumed his work.

Tomorrow the *Evolo* would launch.

***

The Experiment: Subject #94 has been isolated within the experiment for 5,260 days. His mental state continues to deteriorate. The Observation's engineering teams have checked his launch calculations. There is no evidence to support either a successful launch or termination of the subject with the ship's ignition.

According to our calculations, in the case of a catastrophic event, the resulting damages to station #94 will affect the surrounding cloaked stations of Subjects #92, #93, #95 and #97. Those stations will be moderately to severely affected, and their experiments will be concluded accordingly.

Dr. Jack Thayer, 07.16.2118

***

It was time.

The ship was on, a hum reverberating off the walls and instruments. Caspian was ready. He had spent the night before curled up in the mess, watching the nebula blur and glimmer through his tears. He had been able to watch the young stars glowing in amorphous amber all morning before saying a last goodbye and heading to the launch bay.

Seated in the ship, he put on his control gloves to operate the helm. He looked up through the ship's window at the centrifuge rings. His jaw tightened.

Now or never. He inhaled. *If you're right, you're on your way— into the stars and away from this prison.*

If you're wrong, you won't feel it. Not for long.

Caspian slipped on the augmented imaging goggles. The helm was now tinted blue, but through the goggles, functions for the ship appeared, illuminated over the helm's console around him.

Gripping the virtual lever for the engine, he began to bring it towards himself when a signal appeared on his comms display.

He was receiving a message. *How? Who?* His hand hovered over the incoming signal, as if it might bite, before accepting the communication.

"*Caspian,*" a voice crackled into the ship. "*It's Mom.*"

He hung his head. *The day I leave is the day I finally lose it?*

He ignored the hallucination and continued to move the lever, activating the engines embedded within the rings. The humming of the rings grew louder as they began a slow revolution around the *Evolo*'s hull. The ship started to slide forward off its mooring prongs.

"*Caspian. It's your mother.*" The voice was pleading, familiar. "I know this is sudden. But I *am* alive and..." It was a moment before she spoke again. "I've been watching you. I can't see you now, but I can see your ship."

Watching? Caspian frowned, glancing through the window of the craft to the high ceilings of the launch bay. *This isn't real.*

He returned his gaze to the rings. As they turned, the thrum of the engines powering up suffused him, a symphony of sound and increasing gravity pressing into his bones. He checked the probability amplitudes on the QED monitor, fermionic lines dancing across the screen. His fingers drummed on his legs as his feet tapped. He refused to look at the comm.

There was a crackling sound as the voice cleared its throat.

"*Your father and I think you're going to die if you launch. He felt you should be left to make your own choices, but I wanted...*" The voice broke off.

"*I'm sure you have questions—you're part of a great experiment meant to help us understand the amazing things people like you can do with the right tools and education, even if they're left alone in space. Our exploration of the universe, our place amongst the*

*stars—the path you've been on, being raised to be self-sufficient—
you're very important, you know."*

Her voice was meant to be placating, but sounded thin. Pressed for
time and patience. He remembered that tone from when she tried
to get him to hold still for shots as a kid. He had stopped watching
the rings and was staring at the comms monitor instead. He stared
at the waveforms of her voice undulating—they were something.
More than a memory. Somewhere inside him, as he watched the
lines of audio lift and fall, the horror of her words began to take
hold. He felt numb, as if he'd descended miles into himself and
had to use a set of long-range relays just to reach his mouth.

"Caspian, if you don't stop those rings, you will most likely die."

Caspian looked up. The primary ring was spinning faster, the
force of its energy had moved the ship. When it reached a certain
point, the secondary ring would initiate, positioning the engines
for the ship so that it would fall forward. *According to my calculations.* He frowned to himself.

"Please, Caspian. You've done so well. I don't want to see all of
this wasted. There's so much more to discover."

His fingers flexed, sending artificial sensations prickling along
his haptic-gloved hands. Somewhere in the back of his mind,
over the last several minutes, a small part of him was already fan-
tasizing about reuniting with his parents. It was an alteration of
a dream he'd had many times before but had always dismissed:
they'd had amnesia but finally remembered him. Then somehow, they would find their way back to him. They would pick up
where they'd left off. Everything would be fine.

But he was nothing but data—an accomplishment or a failure.
Not a person.

"Caspian!" Susan shouted.

The ring's energy was singing at a higher pitch now. Caspian could feel it in every muscle. The *Evolo* was positioned for take-off. The secondary rings were almost ready. They would be ready as soon as he engaged them, that is. But he had to know—

"Did you ever love me?"

He winced as he heard himself ask this, almost spitting it through clenched teeth. He knew the answer. If he'd been loved, he wouldn't have been left.

"I loved you," Susan said flatly. "I care for *all* my children throughout the experiment. You are not an exception. I know you feel this was cruel, but that's only because you don't understand yet. We knew what was best. We've learned so much from your time on your station—"

This woman wasn't coming to rescue him.

Caspian's eyes narrowed. He pulled up the course for Cepta.

"Wait a few more years. Please. We can meet you. We'll debrief you, apply details of your situation to future experiments. There's so much I want to tell you," Susan paused before she affected a more tender tone. "You've been so brave, my boy."

The secondary ring indicator had begun to glow a minute before but now it was a beacon warning him to initiate or get torn apart by the mounting energy of the first ring. It truly was now or never. But now—family was an option. Mother would meet him. He'd see her, find answers—*continue to be a part of her observations.*

Follow her path. *Again.*

A barrage of memories flowed past him as his breath rasped

shallow in his throat. Mother, running. Father, lecturing. The morning he woke up alone. Reading stories to the nebula. All his days of screaming into empty hallways, tearing things apart. Bloody knuckles where he'd beaten an airlock door when he was twelve, so desperate to escape, to not be on his own any longer.

His breath was a panting staccato, inhaling the ship's tin-tasting air. He tried to stop himself from blacking out. He pulled out an oxygen mask he'd prepared by the command console.

He closed his eyes. He thought of the nebula and her family, of the distance that existed between the station and the hydrostatic center of the gas cloud. He thought of the protostars, unfeeling and unknowing. They weren't his family any more than the woman speaking with him now and in that instant, Caspian aged a decade.

"I'm choosing my own path, Mother."

He closed the comms and with one raised glove descending onto the engine light, he engaged the secondary rings. The ship's hum turned into a howl as it fell forward, approaching the open bay doors.

As the centrifuge rings swirled about in their ever-increasing momentum, the *Evolo* flew out into the dark field of stars, soft and silent.

The course locked, Caspian leaned back from the console, removing his gloves and goggles. The gravity generated by the rings was no longer compounded with the station's. He stretched his arms over his head, fingers brushing storage compartments above him. Shrinking back into his seat, he cast a dark look at the screen beside him. He wanted to raise the comms again, hale his mother, but no.

There would be time for that in the coming years, to interrogate and lay bare his hurt and awakening sense of rage, but only once he was truly under way. He needed to be unable to turn back from the direction he had set before they spoke next. He needed to be untraceable.

Entering the living section in the stern of the ship, he could see his nebula. The *Evolo* was at full speed and had already gained enough distance from the station that it had disappeared. It shouldn't have, but it was as if some kind of optical shielding had engaged now that he was at a distance.

The nebula was more beautiful and so much bigger than he'd thought. The two stars in the heart of the cloudy iridescence were staring back at him, smaller and smaller as the ship sped away, the nebula stretching further upwards and downwards as more of her came into view, a rainbow tear in the fabric of the dark universe. He had spent his whole life following her, as he had Susan, orbiting and observing, never choosing.

He placed his hand on the window in farewell before he sat down. He took a deep breath, an expanse of peace welling up within his chest

My path. My story.

He picked up a book and set his eyes on the window at the helm.

The stars seemed to slip and streak past him as he moved on, heading towards freedom, heading into the dark unknown.

Clouds in her Eyes

Glenna Anne Turnbull

Glenna is a writer/photographer/stained glass artist who lives in the beautiful Okanagan Valley of BC, Canada. Her short fiction has appeared in numerous North American literary magazines. She is currently looking for representation for two very different novels.

Isabella Rodriguez de Fernandos sits still as a cat, perched on an ornate drawing room chair. If she possessed a tail, the very tip of it would be twitching. She stares out the window behind the painter-boy, watching as a small wisp of a cloud begins to extend itself into the starkly naked horizon.

SCRRRRRRRRRITCHHHHHHH — his stiff brush rakes across her dress, recreating its velvety texture in a glistening sheen of oil. She imagines it's the cloud she hears scratching its way across the sky, like a ball of steel wool scouring the color from a porcelain blue bowl.

With jabbing strokes, he pokes pearls into place, encircling her neck like a noose. He knows to paint them bigger than life, like the diamond on her fourth finger and the opal brooch pinned to her chest right where her heart should be. He picks up his pallet knife and begins scraping indifference into her green feline-shaped eyes, then blackens her barely-focused pupils. He knows she's destined to become just another portrait on the family wall.

The cloud begins growing darker in front of Isabella's eyes, becoming opaquer with each dig of the painter's knife. He adds more red to his palette and selects his finest brush, ready to tightly seal her lips, flawless in line for eternity.

Innate fear rumbles inside Isabella and a low growl begins to rise up through her throat.

"May I stretch my legs, please." It's not a question.

The painter-boy's hand freezes, his brush hovering over her lips as Isabella springs from the chair.

She stumbles towards the window, not looking at the sweaty artist or his three-legged easel, her eyes now so clouded she can barely see, her throat so tight from the fumes of his oils she is gasping for air.

The painter-boy lowers his brush and wipes his brow with a rag stained in a cacophony of color. He sighs. He'd been so close to finishing her off. "Well, then Ma'am, will you excuse me while I get a drink?"

Isabella does not answer, does not watch as he scurries from the room like a rat. She reaches her pale arms out in panic, groping to unlatch the window. She pulls on the handles with every inch of her body, the catch releases its hold, and the wind comes swirling in. It spins her in a whirl and she tumbles into the canvas, merging with it, then the wind picks her up and she soars out the window like a kite.

She's frightened at first. The worry lines he'd carved into her forehead begin to deepen. *Help me, I can't fly*, she cries as the wind hooks into the tightly-twisted bun on top of her head and starts pulling her along. Her crushed velvet dress flutters crimson around her limbs. She reaches to grab onto it and watches, horrified, as the Bible he'd painted into her hand falls, plunging the rules to the ground. She grabs hold of the wooden frame she's been crucified onto, gripping the sides for dear life as she climbs higher and higher into the late August sky.

Over the garden wall she goes. Sunflowers nod their clown-like heads to the master's wife as she soars by. Isabella screams to the willow trees that stand guard like sentinels along the private lane but the trees just creak merrily and continue to frolic in the wind, waving good-bye to Isabella with their long branches as if she were a ship setting sail.

Anxiety engulfs her as she looks for someone to reel her in. She spots her husband below, hunting pheasants with the dogs and his gun. She calls out but he doesn't hear her. She's always been silent in his eyes; just a pretty face he might like to mount on his wall.

Westward to the country she flies, completely out of control. *There must be something I can do,* she thinks, completely unfamiliar with what it means to take action. Below her lies a golden field of corn stretched out like a straw mat. She takes a deep breath, then, like a bird, turns her canvas on edge and begins to spiral awkwardly down.

A young woman walking in the field doesn't notice the portrait falling like a bullet-riddled goose from the sky. Her mind is racing, her body walking quickly trying to keep up. She's pretending to look for a lost cat so she can lose herself in her thoughts, free from the prattling of her uncle who says he knows what's best for her. She knows the tall stalks of corn hold the answers if she can only hear their whispers, their silky husks that rustle as quietly as bridal lace dragging across the wooden floor of a church.

The painting comes down with a thud — there is no graceful touchdown for Isabella's first attempt at a three-point landing. The young woman moves through the cornrows towards the sound. She parts the thick stalks and finds Isabella staring up at the sky with startled, unfocused eyes.

She reaches down and picks Isabella up. The thick oil smell catches in her throat as she scans Isabella from head to foot. The scarlet dress is laced so tightly she appears stuffed like a trophy hunter's prize. Similar to the branding on a cow, the monstrous ring on the older woman's finger labels and tags her as something destined to be penned in. Is this the fate that will trap the girl if she consents to her uncle's wishes? She scans Isabella's face for an answer, seeing only bitter green eyes saturated in loneliness and ringed with sadness — eyes that no longer see clearly.

Isabella remembers her younger self, searching for similar answers once upon a time. She squeezes with all her might until red from her dress bleeds onto the girl's hands, warning her, *Run! Run away! And don't be afraid to fly.*

Thank you, the young woman says, grabbing hold of the painting and heaving it back into the sky.

The jolt back into the air loosens Isabella's bun and the confining hairclips can no longer hold against the persuasion of the wind. Isabella's hair unfurls and flows like ribbons. She blinks and her eyes begin to clear as she races on to catch up with the cloud, no longer afraid of flying solo. Warmth from her dress spreads color into her cheeks and the harsh wrinkles the painter-boy had etched so deeply around her mouth and between her brows start to soften with the wind's caress.

She sails on, closer and closer to the sea where the salt air makes her hair curl and the smell reminds her of days spent building castles and dancing with seagulls, free from chains around her neck and manacles on her fingers. Back before she had become just another pretty face. It makes her feel alive.

Along the coastline she dips, Isabella's kite body coasting free for the first time in decades. She's no longer someone's niece, someone's wife or someone's mother, just a shimmering oil image of the woman she has always wanted to be.

The seashore is quiet on this late summer afternoon — no children with brightly painted pails, just an old woman staring out to sea, her smile as unreadable as the Mona Lisa. Isabelle gently swoops down and lands on the bench beside her.

It's my husband, you see. He drowned in this bay so many years ago.

Isabella watches as the woman's eyes begin to water, a stream of tears that flood down her black dress and pool on the bench before trailing down into the ocean. So many tears fall that the tide begins to rise when it should be waning.

Why not send him a note, then, and let him know?

Isabelle watches as the old woman places a note into a bottle and heaves it over the waves. It bobs up and down like an Adam's apple as it drifts off towards her dead husband. The old woman's tears stop and she nods as Isabella tilts forward to catch the next breeze.

As Isabella takes flight, she waves to her and yells, *If you see him, tell him I love him. Tell him I still remember.*

As Isabella streaks out over the ocean, her clothing slides away and she breathes deeply, no longer encumbered by the tight laces, girdle and bustier. The water calls out to her. *Drop*, it says. *Drop into our lap and we will catch you and hold you in our light.*

Isabella slowly dips one corner into the ocean, then the other. Seaweed softly wraps around her limbs to protect her from the coolness of the water. Soon she is submerged to her waist. Her arms break free and she raises them up over her head and dives, breaking away from the canvas to cascade down into the sea in a flurry of colour.

Starfish of the most vibrant purple imaginable come to dance with her hair. Oysters retrieve their pearls from her neck and replace them with a garland of kelp, green as her eyes. She watches as the canvas that had given her life begins to drop away, rocking softly towards the bottom of the sea. Down it spirals towards the corpse of a brokenhearted man trapped by the belief he's unloved and has been forgotten. The man politely tips his head to Isabella. She tells him of the woman sitting on shore and her undying love. The last of the colors from her journey — the red that once threatened to seal her lips forever — floods into his heart and he swims away with a school of fish to find the bottled letter.

Isabella rises to the surface and floats on top like a leaf. Sienna from her skin melds with the forest green of her eyes and ochre brown of her hair, swirling together in the gentle, rhythmic shifts of the tide. She feels a bliss she's never known before. The sunset gets lured into the mix, joining her to form a kaleidoscope of colors.

She knows the painter-boy would tell anyone who'd listen: it was the wind that caused Isabella Rodriguez de Fernados to fly out the window that afternoon. Yes, he would say, it was the wind.

So clearly, only the wind could fix things.

It begins with a gentle ripple — water rings caused from a small splash made by the sun tucking itself into the sea for the night. It progresses to a soft rocking as she lays on her back counting each star that appears. Then she hears it: hushed murmurs of a breeze telling her it's time to go home.

Fragments of her soul begin to climb back into the atmosphere, riding shotgun on the water that had cradled her so softly. As the wind builds, more and more of Isabella fills the sky like paper lanterns until every inch of her is buoyant in the night air. It begins to gust as she bonds herself back together, storming higher, faster, devouring everything in her path, sucking in knowledge like a cyclone — this is true love, this is compromise, this is what it means to take action. She pulls and hoards, reining it all inside of herself. She examines the resentment, the hatred and abuse she's known, smashing through the fences of expectation that had once held her bound. Into her garden and right up the wall she rages with a flash of lightning then beats her fists down on the shutters, her fingernails clattering on the panes like hail until finally, the window flings open again and she turns and walks back to her chair.

The painter boy returns to the room, his glass re-filled with water. He reaches over to close the window, unaware of the starfish dancing in her hair or the night stars that shine in Isabella's cleared eyes. "Okay. Please take your position so we can finish."

She begins to smile, her lips stubbornly open, and bares her teeth.

Face

A. Mills Klipstine

Amy Mills Klipstine is a Los Angeles-based fiction writer and screenwriter who loves all things speculative. She is currently earning her MFA in Creative Writing from Antioch University Los Angeles.

"I have a face laid waste."

Marguerite Duras

Welcome to Mother Mal's Elixir Den. May the sun shine upon you no more.

I sing this to the woman with the leather face who stands outside the door. She arrived just after dawn, hidden behind a velvet robe of the deepest purple, carrying only a change purse clutched by spindly bones. Not knocking, no, but waiting, for it is my job to let her in ever since Lita left. Without Lita . . . without Lita it is I who must usher in the desperate. The desperately old, but rich, of course, for they all come to see Mother Mal to get their faces fixed. But no one can fix a face, can they? And if it is fixed, why do they return? These are questions I would ask Lita, should have asked Lita, before she went away.

Come in so Mother may bless you, I say to the woman. She nods, the folds of her hood sliding away to reveal her face, dry, yellowed. The stretching has pulled skin so taut I can run fingers along it without hitting a bump. But that is never the worst. No, the worst is always the eyes—endlessly deep caverns, ready to swallow you as punishment for staring too long. If eyes are a pathway to the soul, as Lita used to say, then souls do not come to see Mother Mal.

A puff of air escapes the jagged crack of the woman's mouth, pouring out odors sour and foul. Smells live here too; you get used to it after a while.

She glides past me into our den. I slide my tattered slipper until it sits just outside the door—as far as I will ever go—to peer down the alley. Tendrils of fog snake up the stone walls, lingering on the crumbling patches where weeds have pushed through. Distant echoes of carts and passersby trickle down the cobblestones, carrying word of citizens going about the business of living.

A chill dances across my neck, rousing my hairs. Is it an illusion, or is someone standing there, just down the alley, a figure tucked into shadow and fog? Watching the entrance to Mother Mal's Elixir Den?

I resist the urge to call out to it. I slip back inside, close the door, and click the latch. The living have no place here.

My face leads me as I shuffle the woman along Mother's hall of mirrors. Lita used to say that mirrors are a reminder of why you are here. Mirrors give you the courage to do what you must. What must my face do? It is round and puffy, red and shiny. My face is growing just as it should, Mother Mal always tells me. So I let it grow. Maybe one day it will grow so big it will float me out of the shop and into the sky toward Lita, wherever she is.

The mirror hallway guides us toward a towering gilded arch, like a tongue pulling us to the open mouth of Mother's den, where the stairs of her spine spiral us down deeper and deeper into the earth toward Mother's belly, below any basement in Marjoran, below the base of the mountain that frames the city to the east.

The sun is skin's great evil, Mother Mal always says, and no sun can follow us down here. No mayors. No sentry, either. Mother's den is below all of those rules and customs. Only those who know can find us, and the number of those who know only grows as the years upon them do.

The damp earth jiggles as we descend, feet pounding the metal stairs, one clank after another, signaling to Mother we have come. She sings in response, a slow and sweet ballad sung in the old days of Marjoran before the war. The song lifts up the woman who trails me, filling her with life, breathing into her chest and pushing out hums perfectly in tune. Mother has a gift for memory, returning the lifeless to a time of wonder.

Welcome, welcome, to Mother Mal's Den. You come to renew yourself again.

Mother starts to sing a new tune—her welcoming song. To this I can hum along, I know this one in the depths of my belly for Lita used to hum it as she worked, me at her feet, catching her shavings as she scrubbed the walls.

Welcome all who grow into the night. You come full of sorrow but leave a delight.

Mother's voice is deep and heavy, and it slides down my throat like spiced mint tea, warming my insides and coaxing me further into the earth. The woman and I follow, silently, led by Mother's song, until the stairs empty us into her den—a massive cavern, the ceiling lost above us in the darkness where light can't reach. Along the walls sit kerosene torches, their fires casting flickering hues of orange and yellow that flit across intricately woven tapestries in all colors of the world above. In the middle stands Mother Mal, a glowing jewel in her beaded gown, stirring the cauldron over the stone fire pit, each swish of the bubbling liquid a punctuating note in her tune.

Welcome all for winter's come. Welcome all to come undone.

We stop just before the offering mat, woven from golden fibers, set to entice those to give, as Lita used to say. Mother Mal does not look at us. Her satin gown alive from the torchlight, rows of beads and sequins each fighting for their tiny glint. Always so beautiful, Mother is. Lita used to say Mother has the most beautiful face. I know the woman behind me thinks so. I can feel the intensity of her desire wiggle past me like a worm, heading to the fire to be reborn. For you cannot be reborn without fire.

You are late.

Mother speaks slowly, just above a whisper, but the disapproval finds me and sticks to my skin. Lita would not be so slow.

I leave you, Mother, I say and step away.

Not today, Uma. Today, you stay.

I have never watched an elixir be born. Was always Lita. I was the scullery, the cloth my life, my only purpose to keep Mother's Den a sparkling gem. I was content to be forgotten, always behind Lita, safely within her shadow. The cruelty of Lita's absence, of what I must do, forms in my mind, a taunting shadow.

Mother turns to us, and I hear the woman's gasp. Mother's face is pure magic. The edges puffed, the valleys smooth, skin like the first dusting of snow upon the ground. Her eyes, however, are not their usual sparkling green but dimmed, slightly, since Lita left.

The woman falls to her knees on the offering mat. Her bones crackle in response, pushed to a limit.

Oh, Mother. Give. *Give.* Please, I beg. Give me one more. Just one more.

The woman scrapes her fingers across her face, tracing lines and cracks that have burrowed roots. These cracks grew on our journey down, as if she descended not to our cave but to an awaiting tomb.

Lita always warned me not to watch the cracks.

Bursts of sobs push up from the woman's body, now bent in prayer. The elixir in the pot bubbles in response, stronger, heavier, ready to consume. Hisses whiz past my ears, and I imagine the memories trapped here are weeping with her, their wails pushing through the earth to join the rising steam of the elixir, adding their agony to its growing hunger.

I never wanted to watch. Lita never let me. But Lita is gone.

Mother Mal sweeps past to the crouched woman, her dress flowing on a breeze born of purpose. One lean hand is placed upon the heaving shroud.

Shhh, my child. Shhh.

Mother starts humming again, the old tune, weighted with history, hopes and dreams, terrors and sorrows. Mother's song awakens the past, the bits of my life before bought me and brought me to the den, and I can remember the city, its shining glass spires and polished metal roofs, the whizzing of airships, the crowded streets of merchants, where I once hid, my job to steal scraps for the day.

My mind hums along, finding its place in the tune, following behind as it pitches higher and higher, up and up until the final trill leads to the fall, like the dawn past a night. The woman has stopped sobbing. Her face raises up to Mother, like a child, her child, come home.

Why have you come again? Mother asks.

Youth and beauty have left me. The woman's voice is but a creak.

What is the beauty of youth?

Eternity.

What are you willing to pay for eternity?

Everything.

The opening ritual complete, Mother stands and places an arm around my shoulder. Her closeness, not warm, but frigid, its icicles dripping down my sides, shaking my knees.

Uma, come, to the fire.

The steady embers of the fire keep the cauldron's contents a smoking heap, the pop and hiss of bubbles still resounding. Something foul seeps out, like old cheese, rotted fish, and burnt flesh. My nose itches from the steam that carries the stench. I used to smell it on Lita's clothes after the rituals. She wouldn't let me see her. Never could I see her. Not for days. But her clothes would be left in a pile for me to clean until she could return to the world, her face redder, tighter, used. Lita would never speak about the burning, only that Mother had taken and that it was our job to give.

How many years I watched pour over Lita until one day, she was no more. Her very existence but a memory, one that fades.

Now it is my turn to give, Mother has told me. I am not ready,

I realize, as my limbs beg to break free and run up the stairs to breathe the air above, away from the smoky haze of Mother's belly.

Mother is singing again, her deep voice louder, heavier.

We give, we take, ourselves we make.

The woman starts singing along, and the flames jump and pop to the urgent melody, ready to devour the cauldron.

Mother takes my hand in hers. I can feel the barren waste between the rough-hewn edges of her palm, like leather left out to rot in the midday sun. The lie is always revealed by the hands, Lita would say. Mother's hands are a lie, and mine start to quiver.

I do not want to, I say. Mother sings louder, drowning me out.

We give, we take, ourselves we make.

I do not want to follow Mother. I want to return to the kitchens, where mold and mildew were my friends, my endless scrubbing for purity among the rusted silver my only thought. I was brought here for this, Mother has said, and I cannot leave until Mother wills it or a worse fate awaits me in Marjoran's prisons. But I always had Lita to guide me, hold me, brush my hair and help me learn my way about the caves. Never was I a part of Mother's rituals. Never had I spoken with her visitors. They come from all across Marjoran and even beyond, across the Saltis Sea, as far as the Barren Lands of the West.

Mother has both of my hands trapped underneath the rubble of hers. We are headed toward the cast iron cauldron and its smoking depths. Heat pours from the lip, uncomfortable heat. I will melt if I get closer, I know.

We give, we take, ourselves we make.

We stand over the pot, the hiss, cackle, pop, groan. Noises flood my face, push down my throat, burning a path to my belly. I can feel tendrils snake within me, reaching for something I don't want to give. My hands are in the liquid now, searing heat racing up my skin, melting it away. I want to scream from the pain, but I can't, I can only cry, for worse than the heat, and the burning, and the melting, is the sorrow. Something is being taken. Something from deep within my bones. I feel it leave with the heat, pouring out of me with my breath, leaving only darkness.

Cold stone on my cheek.

My body lies on the polished black slate of Mother Mal's den. Have I slept? Have I died and returned?

All I know is that Mother Mal is done with me. I can feel my face deflate, one less breath of life from within me. I open my eyes and see my hands splayed before me—raw, bloody, skin hanging in tatters, only portions left that cling to bone. There is no more pain, only waste.

They regrow, you know, I hear Lita say in my head, at first they regrow.

I sit up, my tunic looser than it was before, as if part of my body was taken. I watch as my skin smoothes over sharp edges, filling in cracks and bringing back life, filling out my hands, tightening once again around my fingers, but yet no sensation.

What happens when they don't regrow, I had asked Lita. My voice small then, still unformed. Did she answer? I cannot remember.

Mother Mal turns to the woman. I have given you my dearest. What are you willing to give?

I am not Mother's dearest. Lita was her dearest.

I bring you my fondest memory, the woman says. Her face is wet, liquid seeping from her dark caverns.

Only that which you most admire.

Yes, Mother.

What you must pay to be admired.

Yes, Mother.

The woman lifts up her hands in prayer.

We give, we take, ourselves we make.

The singing is so loud it bounces off the stone, following Mother back to the cauldron where she scoops elixir into a glass jeweled jar, carrying it to the woman, cupped in her hands like an offering. The woman must drink. She must ingest what has been given.

Now you give to me, Mother says.

The woman lifts up her hands and Mother pours the liquid into her open mouth. At first, nothing, not even a swallow, but then I see it, escaping, a thin yellow cloud pulsating, alive. It slithers from the woman's mouth and weaves through the air, growing, glowing, sending an energy that feels light, almost joyous.

A memory.

It flits through the air above me, and I catch its tail, pulling myself in.

A hand tickles my belly as I roll in the grass, bright green, damp and dew-crusted, the smell of fresh dirt invading my lungs. I lie in tall grass, but not alone, and I laugh and laugh. Hands wrap around my stomach and pull me close, a hand now around my neck, edging me forward to soft lips. I let myself relax and my body tingles, alive. I open my eyes and see deep, rich brown eyes peering back. Somewhere birds are conversing, and wind whips leaves like a flutter of trumpets, but this kiss is all I want, and it lasts while my body melts into the ground.

Words of love, promises, a future, impossible words but true, carrying feelings that breathe into my skin and all I know is I want to stay here and feel this love.

I must hold on to this. Forever.

The memory slips through my fingers, lost. It snakes into Mother's open mouth, filling her up like the airships that glide above the city in the clouds. And then, gone, as quickly as it came.

Love. Peace. I have never known either, only soap and water on black stone, straw mats, tattered shirts, the food scraps Mother won't eat. How I long for the light. But the memory was never mine. It was hers. Now a piece of this woman is gone, into Mother where it doesn't belong. I look at the woman's hunched form bent at sharp angles underneath her purple robes. A heaving mass, groaning, growing, until she stands, and her hood drops away from her face.

A glorious face.

The hollow eyes have defined into a sea of blue waves with white crests, her skin puffed out, red hot, a newborn entering the world. But her joy is gone. That love I felt, I cannot see in her newborn eyes. Why did she let it go?

I hold up my hands, framing her face within my open palms. We are the same. Her face is me.

We give, we take, ourselves we make.

Mother continues singing, one open palm held out. The woman hands over a shining signet ring, a ruby, perhaps, and Mother places it on the shelf next to other once-valuable trinkets. But this is not the real payment, no. I try to recreate the woman's memory in my mind, to haul it in, to make it mine. Grass and wind and kisses. But the feeling is gone. It is in Mother, somewhere, kept alive. What does she do with them, the memories? Do they keep her warm?

Mother says no more, so I lead the woman back out of the belly and up the stairs. The mirrors await, but I do not let myself look. I do not let myself see my face. Yet it walks with me, following me.

The door is heavy; I must use my entire body to pull it open, the gold handle digging into the raw skin of my hands, sending ripples up my wrists. The woman pushes past me, then pauses in the doorway, blue eyes peering into my face.

You gave it away.

The woman only nods.

Is it worth it?

She touches her cheek, and I touch mine in response. Is it hard? Rough? I cannot feel yet, my fingers are sticks pulled from dead trees.

She leaves.

I want to live in the love she gave away. Will she try to get it back now? Will she chase it into the night with her new face?

The woman disappears down the alley, her robe trailing behind her. As I watch her leave, my eyes drift to just past the crook where the alley turns west. The sun has pushed through the fog revealing the figure, still there in the corner. Tall, unmoving, wearing a red hooded cape. The hood falls away and the face is old, wrinkled, sunken, eyes bulging and red. A beggar, it is. Mother has talked of those. Beware the beggars, Uma, they bring only death, she said. The beggar takes one step, then another, hands reaching out toward me as if wanting to grab hold and drag me into darkness.

I scream, I think, I'm not sure. The hands, skeleton's bone, reaching, reaching, the wind whipping white spindly hair so the wisps stand like snakes upon the beggar's head. I will turn to stone if I linger here.

I haul myself against the door, push it across the tiles, cringing as the hinges screech until the door shuts with a thud.

***

Dancing in the firelight. I'm dancing, dancing, round in circles, the layers of my dress spinning, beads slapping each other in the frenzy, hands clapping somewhere nearby. The fire roars higher, my hands rise to match its strength. There's happiness here somewhere and I'm dancing to meet it.

Lita is with me, her laughter coming in ripples. She's glorious. Not the Lita who Mother stole, slowly, but the Lita I first met when Mother bought me. Long, wavy midnight hair, smooth face, eyes lit by fire. She's holding my hand, pulling me around the fire; together we twirl and twirl. This is love, I think. This is what it feels like.

Come with me, she says.

How?

Something cold approaches me from behind. Creeping up from the depths of the lake, snaking around my ankles, trying to pull me down. Lita pulls back. Keep dancing, she says, never go down, never look, keep dancing to the fire.

The fire, a lion, roars and grows, pawing the sky. She pulls me closer, closer until I'm almost inside the lion, ready to burn.

I gasp as I wake, my chest constricted, frozen in place, not willing to expand for another breath. Pressure on my back, a stone, a weight. My face deflates again, I can feel it closing in upon my bones. Something is sucking me dry, like a slow leak in a balloon, the hiss escaping out of me, somewhere.

Shhh. The calming voice slides like soap across my wet back.

Shhh, says Mother. I know it's her. Seated next to me, on the floor, beside my straw mat.

Mother has never come for me in my sleep. She used to come for Lita. I remember the nights. I would first wake to the sounds— soft scrapes against stone, a moaning wind somewhere near—a monster approaching, I thought, my eyes clasped tight, my body cold with fear. Lita's gasp still rings in my ears, mingled with my own, the soft humming from somewhere nearby. I would never look. Lita told me never to look.

But even here in the cellar, in the deepest cave of all of Marjoran, I am still within Mother's reach.

My face moves on its own, having been summoned. Mother is above me, her hand on my back, face glowing as if the moon resides within her. Coming in waves, her humming, landing on my cold skin and sliding off, unable to comfort.

She is taking. I feel myself bleed onto the blanket, something of myself oozing out of a wound. Mother's face, mouth ajar, teeth like razors, coming for me. I close my eyes and think of the fire; can I summon it? I want to follow you, Lita, I want to burn.

* * *

Welcome to Mother Mal's Elixir Den. May the sun shine upon you no more.

I sing the song, now familiar, now mine.

Days move one into the next. Mother's belly swells with visitors, one a week, handing Mother baubles that she hoards in piles, crowding the cavern shelves. But even more, giving Mother their memories. Where does she hoard those? Do they sit, unused, unloved, in piles upon the shelves of her ribcage?

I try to hold on to the memories, when I can, before they are consumed by Mother. The birth of a child. The kiss of a lover. The warmth of a mother's embrace. All things I have never known. Wisps I grab onto, hold tight, imprint what I can onto my soul, like tiny stamps upon the surface, infusing me with seconds of joy until they float away.

I will never understand why they are given. Once a memory leaves, what happens in the space that is left behind? Is it a hole, a tear in ourselves, unable to be filled?

I only have memories of Lita to hold on to, Lita, cold nights, and Mother's song.

The front door is heavy today, each day a little more, my bones creak with the burden of it. Outside, the day's heat sticks to the skin, the sun already seeking me from over the top of the alley wall, wanting to take more of what little is left. The beggar is not here. Usually they are there, just past the crook, hunched in the dark, like a nagging thought of things once forgotten trying to break through.

The woman standing before me today has not been here before, that much she has told me. Her blood-red robe hides her face from me, only visible are her hands of skeleton bone grasping the robe closed, holding in herself.

They all hide when they come. Only once they leave do women let in the light.

We make our way down the long hall, the mirrors taunting me with their truth. I will not look. I will not see my face. Mother says it is still growing, just as it should. But I know better. I can feel the hollowness of my cheeks like the sand after a retreating wave.

The woman shuffles behind me, each step sounding like a burden. Deeper we go, down the stairs to where Mother waits. The visitor is slow today, slower than most. But still, she follows. No one retreats. No price is ever too high. That's what has depressed my spirit most, knowing that no memory, no part of oneself, is ever too valuable to not throw away.

Would I give up Lita? Holding my hand as we drift asleep. Whispering in my ear when I cry at night.

Mother's song drifts up the stairs to greet us. Her hum rises and falls in long trills, flowing through my memory, awakening my mind. This song is one I've heard often, back when Lita would dust Mother's valuables on the shelf and I would catch the flying particles once they hit the floor, wiping the stone until my cloth pulled apart. I used to think it was just for us, a secret song, a way to speak her thanks as we rubbed our fingers red. But since Lita left, I have not heard the tune.

Mother never once asked after Lita. Never once did Mother

venture out into the world to seek her. Never once spoke her name other than the morning I awoke, cold and alone, with Mother sitting next to me, her cold hand placed upon my forearm, her cracked voice whispering, It's just us now.

Just us.

The woman behind me begins to hum in unison, her voice a scratch as it races to catch the notes on their journey. I find myself matching her, singing along, as if I'm back on the ground, rubbing stone, Lita's bare feet standing before me.

We enter the den. Mother waits beside the cauldron, her face aglow. I've never seen her look so fresh and full, her skin puffed out and glinting, wet stone after a rain. She stops humming, her arms open wide in greeting, the song pouring from her lips.

Welcome, welcome, to Mother Mal's Den. You come to renew yourself again.

Welcome all who grow into the night. You come full of sorrow but leave a delight.

Welcome all for winter is come. Welcome all to come undone.

Mother's voice grows, and I realize the woman is singing along, her voice high and tinny. The words flow out of her, as if in a trance. I search for her face, hidden beneath her robes. But it's only a dark crevice, her sound escaping a black hole.

Mother stops and silence falls upon the den. The woman falls to the floor, red robe billowing about her like a puddle of blood. Her hands still clutch the hood, her face hidden. But I can feel the years upon her like a stone weight, pushing her into the ground, coaxing her to leave the world.

Why have you come? Mother asks, moving forward, slowly, one

foot, then another, the beads of her dress glinting in the torch-light, clinking as she steps.

Youth and beauty have left me, Mother.

What is the beauty of youth?

Eternity.

What are you willing to pay for eternity?

What am I willing to pay...The woman's voice drifts. My chest clenches with the wait. The ritual is always the same, no questions, no faltering. But this woman falls away, not finishing her thought.

Mother takes another step forward, then places her hand on the woman's back. I can see the woman's shudder send ripples across the fabric.

What are you willing to pay for eternity?

A sigh escapes the woman, deflating her body even more, shrinking her into the earth.

Everything.

It has been spoken. The ritual shall continue. I haul myself to the cauldron, not needing Mother to call me. Not needing her stare to warn me of my duty.

We give, we take, ourselves we make.

Mother sings but this is my song now. This is my payment. I give. They take. My self is remade each time, older, I know, but also something gone. Something inside me vacates with each ritual. Like a knife scraping butter from its block to be spread and consumed by others.

The woman in red hands something to Mother, something small and shiny. A ring perhaps. I can feel the woman's eyes, from somewhere within the depths of her hood, watch me as Mother approaches the cauldron, singing her song.

I look up into Mother's face. Is it Mother's? Is it mine? My face that once followed me down the hall of mirrors. My face that used to be kissed by Lita.

Mother does not smile. What does she see when she looks at me? For a moment, I detect a sluice of sadness slide across her pupils. Is there regret there, somewhere, of what I must do? Does Mother regret? I want to ask, but I have never asked Mother a question such as this. That is not my place. Mother found me, a lost child, and mother will un-find me, one day, this I know in my bones.

Sing it, Uma. Sing it so she hears.

We give, we take, ourselves we make.

I sing as my hands go into the cauldron. I sing as the pain unceasingly stabs like an army of bees. I sing as my skin slides down my arms. I sing as I feel my very insides turn to liquid and chase after my heartbeat as it bleeds out down my fingers into the pot. I sing even as I hear the woman behind me sing along, lifting her voice to match mine as it falters.

We give, we take, ourselves we make.

Give it to me. The woman is screaming now, above the song, above the hissing of the cauldron as it releases its steam. Give it to me. I deserve it back. I gave and gave.

And now you take, Mother says.

I fall to the floor, my life seeping onto the stone. I can hear the clanking glass of the vial. The slooping of the liquid. Mother's footsteps clicking against the stone. The memory will come if I can wake for it. The memory is all I have to keep me going. A ray of warmth until I must die again.

I cannot feel my face, but somehow I turn my head. The woman in red stands tall, towering above my body, her hood fallen, hair screaming about her head in white waves. It's the beggar, I know it now, her ragged smile and hungry eyes, arms held out, ready to clench my life. She is here but I cannot tell Mother. I cannot tell her what I know.

Mother hands over the vial and the beggar brings it up with shaking hands, liquid oozing down her mouth as she drinks my lifeblood.

Mother watches, her body taut with anticipation. So foreign it is; she never cares for the weary.

The woman closes her eyes, sways. The memory must be coming now. I brace myself for it. Raise up my arm. There it is, coming out, a thin glinting line, so delicate it flutters on the wind like dust that's been disturbed. I spread my fingers to touch the particles that float past, pulling me in.

Dancing. I'm dancing. The black night around me envelops my body, punctuated by blazing orange and red. A fire. I'm dancing by the firelight. I can feel powdery dirt below my bare feet. I can feel laughter rip my chest. I'm laughing with someone who moves beside me, their arms twined with my arms, moving me in circles.

I try to focus on the figure, it's all blurry and confused. I'm dizzy and tired, but so full inside I want to burst.

I see the face, finally, as the movement stops and the white lines slow to spots of stars in the sky. A face, full, round, red, and smooth.

Bushy brows above dark eyes, set wide apart, ready for more. This is my face.

This is my fire.

The face is me and I am with me. I am Lita.

Come with me, my mouth says to my face. When you see me again, you will come with me, Uma.

My memory, I hold.

My...

A sharp gasp pulls me back to the den. Mother is holding my body. I must be crying. She is yelling something. The woman in red is laughing. Her body is moving, dancing, singing.

We give, we take, ourselves we make.

Only, she is not singing to Mother, she is singing to me. Lita is here and I must go with her. She had a face, laid waste, taken by Mother, given to others. She is what I will become. She is where my face is going.

I know now, without really knowing. I somehow stand, push Mother away, and join Lita in her dance. Laughter is here, coming out of me. Lita is here. And she now has my face—cheeks plump as plums, skin brushed by the sun in all its sunset colors, lips puffed and full.

We twirl until the den blurs into a swirl of torchlight and black shadow. She has told me of this, I realize. This is a memory. A whisper into my ear in the night. This is what I could not remember. What she reached out to tell me.

We give, we take, ourselves we make.

I know what to do. Mother knows too, for she is clawing at me, screaming my name, screaming Lita's name, but we grab her, together, singing, together. Mother goes into the cauldron, not just her arms, but all of her, down to the beads at the rim of her gown, all melting into the liquid as Mother seeps away. We drink her in, the whole pot of her, taking back ourselves and leaving her out, until only a soggy gray sludge is left at the bottom.

Mother Mal is gone.

Heat rushes through me, the fire, now inside, as I continue to dance. The memories are in us now, filling our lungs with hot roiling air, taking root in our growing brains. We are a mother, a daughter, a father, a son. We laugh. We play. We fly. We love.

Up we go, hand in hand, Lita has returned, and I let the mirrors show me, all of me, as I used to be, with my face, a dew drop, growing again, just as it should.

We open the door and slip out into the daylight, letting the sun burn its marks across our skin. Lita's hand is in mine, and she pulls me down the alley, away from Mother Mal's Elixir Den, into the streets of Marjoran, where people go about the business of living. Where people are full of Memories ready to be made and kept.

The Time Speaker

Emmie Christie

Emmie Christie's work tends to hover around the topics of feminism, mental health, cats, and the speculative such as unicorns and affordable healthcare. She has been published in Flash Fiction Online and Three-Lobed Burning Eye, and she graduated from the Odyssey Writing Workshop in 2013. She also enjoys narrating audiobooks for Audible. You can find her at www.emmiechristie. com or on Twitter @EmmieChristie33.

Katie had always known the time, down to the second.

A quirk, her mother theorized, from when Katie had toddled around in the yard and gauged how much time she had left to play outside. At 20, her friends guessed she'd trained in punctuality for her acting auditions and made a big deal out of it. Katie liked the attention at first, until Tasha called her up drunk with a timer set up and asked her to "show us the superpower." Katie had laughed it off and said she'd just glanced at her phone, though she hadn't.

She'd always known it was something more.

She'd felt it, in the watches, in the phones, in clocks on the wall. When she visited London for an acting gig and ambled by Big Ben, she shivered all the way to the tips of her fingers. Something whispered to her in a strange language, in ticks and slips of passing moments, and it had amplified as she'd grown, as time became more valuable, as age spots bloomed on her father's hands.

A superpower, her friends had said for years. A superpower, to be hyper aware of the passing of time? Or a curse?

She tried to ignore it. Sometimes it distracted her. And then, while preparing for Shakespeare on the Green one spring, her phone's display of 3:37pm, second 49 unspooled into a word, translating to 'warning,' the same as 'la manzana' meant apple in Spanish.

Katie almost dropped her script. *What*, she thought, *was that?*

***

She puzzled over it on the set for Midsummer Night's Dream. Had her brain dialed into some alien radio frequency? Had the Russians figured out how to project thoughts?

Her director scrunched his eyebrows a few times. "Lines," he'd say. "Get your lines down." And she had. But something else had wormed into her mind, stopping her midsentence. Had something whispered a word at 7:44am, 12 seconds? Yes. 'Father.' It had said 'Father.'

"Can you please keep up?" Her director pressed his pencil against his lips. "We're running out of time."

"Of course, of course. Sorry."

***

She'd ignored her ability most of her life—not really because of irritation with her friends' shenanigans, or because it distracted her, but because it *loomed*, like someone waited for her in a dark alley.

Foreboding had always shadowed her sense of time, a sense of impending . . .

Just that, impending. Like a sentence that wouldn't finish. She watched the time, like a driver watched the road, even on a straight highway with no traffic. Alert. Vigilant. Ready to swerve.

She called her mother on her break. "Is Dad okay? Is anything wrong?"

"He left for the factory the same as always, honey. Why?"

"Just a bad feeling."

Her 'intuition' as her mother called it ended up revealing the tremors in his hands. "Alzheimer's, early stage," the doctors said. Treatments would help, but they could do nothing against the slow march of time.

She cursed at the thing, at the being, at whatever talked to her. "It's your fault. It's your fault. You *caused* this."

It responded with more translations. At 4:59: 'Leader.' At 9:18: 'Heart.'

A superpower. A superpower, to diagnose the inevitable. Or had she caused it? Was her comprehension the catalyst for these emergencies? Was fate so cruel? Maybe if she didn't speak them out loud, nothing would happen.

On the other hand, what if she could prevent a tragedy? The words might not be inevitable. She had to try.

"It's been kind of stressful, lately," she said to her director. "How are you doing health-wise?"

He scrunched his eyebrows as he always did. "Probably should do a checkup. Been a bit out of breath."

***

Just knowing words didn't equal understanding. Time was an older language; it didn't have conjunctions like 'and,' it didn't use modern terms like 'director.'

It helped that she'd listened to it her whole life, however, and soon she learned a new word almost every day. She didn't comprehend Time as a whole on a specific day but awakened to it like the transition from night to sunrise, where the black sky stretched into purples and blues. She translated the words at their corresponding seconds and the entity, or whoever spoke to her, would string together a sentence for her throughout the day.

Her 'superpower' warned when someone's time *could* be cut short. Her director found a small hole in his heart. They fixed it. They did Midsummer Night's Dream without incidence.

A quirk. A curse. A power.

Each second spoke. Each moment held meaning. She helped Tasha find a tumor before it turned malignant. Her father died five years later, but she received no other warnings for him. It was his time, his true time.

It named her the 'Time Speaker.' And to complete the handshake over the cosmos, she asked: "What do you look like?" She wanted to know what spoke to her in the quiet ticks and tocks.

It said once in answer, at 3:49, 11 seconds: "Mother." And then, at 8:12, 45 seconds: 'Sentinel.'

A sentience of seconds transmitting a code out into the universe. Maybe she had spoken for centuries, or millennia. Waiting, just around the corner, in the alley of peoples' minds. Waiting for someone to listen and care, as she, the Sentinel Mother did. A time speaker.

Dinner with Jupiter

Clare Diston

Clare Diston is a writer, editor and
proofreader. She has an MA in Creative
Writing and is currently studying for a
BSc in Astronomy. She is fascinated by
the crossovers between science and art,
and she explores these intersections in
her writing. Her work has appeared
in Capsule Stories, Lazy Women and
The Bohemyth.

There is a point, when you have been alone for a very long time, that you begin to look for company in anything. It begins with your own voice, speaking your thoughts out loud just to free them from the confines of your head, to know that, here at least, you have vibrated the air and made your presence felt. You may move on to personifying inanimate objects: naming your television, making the spatula squeal as you dip its head into boiling sauce, saying 'I love you' to your bed. From there, it's just a matter of time until your inwardness expands outwards and begins to encompass the house, the street, the city, the sky. It is a paradox of loneliness that you can feel both small and unnoticed, and at the same time like the tender, beating heart of the universe.

All this is to say that I had been alone for a very long time when I decided to invite the planets to dinner.

***

It was a summer evening, more than a year into the crisis that had confined all of us to our houses, only able to see each other (and ourselves) through blurred boxes on screens. The doors to my balcony were open—a feeble attempt to freshen up my little one-room flat—but the air was apathetic, so I lay on the sofa, limbs soft, mind exhausted yet restless, watching the sky darken and the first stars blink into light.

It was after nine and I hadn't eaten yet. There were ingredients in the fridge for a fairly elaborate meal, but I could not settle my mind enough to make my limbs do the work of preparing food. A nice meal. Another nice meal. Another pleasant evening at home. Another week of nothing to do, which in previous times I might have called 'relaxing' or 'self-care'. Another, another, another. I pictured the contents of my fridge—red globes of tomatoes, the cratered surface of a wedge of cheese, onions with layers like planets—not six feet away, but as unreachable to me in my inertia as the stars.

There, beyond my balcony, was a real planet, visible against the still-pale summer sky. Venus, probably. Or Mars. A bright pin-point, like a seed.

Eventually hunger won out. For half an hour I moved around my kitchen, pulling the ingredients together into a meal, imagining a breeze on my back. While my dinner simmered on the hob, I went to the little dining table and set out a plate, a knife and fork, a glass of water. It was what I had done on many evenings since I'd lived here, and every evening for the last year since the restaurants were closed—but tonight the table seemed emptier than usual, and I was struck by an urge to decorate it.

Decorating the dinner table—that's something people do on special occasions, or when they're expecting company. But why shouldn't I do it for myself? Why shouldn't I do something nice just because I'm the only person here? There's no reason!

I was determined, but rustling up a table decoration when you haven't planned one is difficult, especially when you don't have the space to keep things that are purely decorative. I was picturing a white tablecloth with a runner of red fabric up the middle, three gold candlesticks, a cut-glass bowl with flowers floating in perfumed water. Scrabbling in my cupboards rewarded me with an old blue tablecloth and three tea-lights in shiny tinfoil casings. It was not the lavish scene I had imagined for myself.

I was just considering fetching the succulents from the book-shelf when the sky beyond my balcony caught my attention. It was properly dark now, and the few brightest stars were shining bravely through the streetlight haze. The planet, Venus or Mars, hovered like a firefly right in front of me.

The planets—now they would be a table decoration. Imagine them all, lined up like gems along my table. They would give me something beautiful to look at while I eat. And if I can't go out underneath the sky, then the least I can do is bring it in to me.

And so, I decided. I went out onto the balcony and leaned over the railing as far as I could, pushing myself up onto my toes and stretching towards the pinprick of light in the sky. The railing dug into my stomach and made me feel a little sick; the five-floor fall yawned beneath me. But after a few seconds of reaching, my fingertips brushed cloud tops, and with one final effort I strained forward and plucked the planet out of the sky.

It was Venus. A smoky marble—pale yellow and slightly stinging to the touch. I rolled it around in my palm for a moment, watched the top layer of clouds swirl and eddy against my skin. Part of me wanted to lick it. My tongue poked out from between my lips; I imagined it would taste sour and sharp, like the sweets you eat as a child that make your lips pucker into a kiss. But I didn't; I put it on the table instead, where it made a dark yellow smudge on the tablecloth.

I went back to the window and let my eyes rove around the sky again, until I found the reddish tint of Mars. This was easier to reach, closer, and when I had it in my hands it felt rough and cool. I rubbed my thumb over the summit of Olympus Mons, sank my fingernail into the trench of Valles Marineris. Then I placed Mars on my table too.

Jupiter came next—large and unwieldy, but not too heavy despite its size. Holding this planet was a joy; my fingers sank into the surface of it a little, and I twisted and turned it to catch the light. Pale blue aurorae rippled around its poles; the Great Red Spot, that enormous, three-hundred-year-old storm, raged near the base of my thumb. I had the same urge to taste Jupiter as I'd had with Venus—it would be creamy, fudgy, swirled like ice cream—but I felt this was too undignified a thing to do to a giant of the Solar System, so I set it down next to the bowl of peas.

I got hold of Saturn by pinching the outer edge of one of its rings and tugging until the planet came within reach. It was quite difficult to hold, encircled by that thin, tiger-striped band of rings, so I gripped it from underneath, my fingers tucked under the rings like an egg cup, with Saturn itself the egg. When I set it down on the table, it leaned over so that one edge of its rings touched the tablecloth, holding the planet at a jaunty angle.

Mercury was quite difficult to find, but when I finally pinched hold of it, it felt warm on one side and cold on the other, like a half-cooked pea. To reach Uranus and Neptune I had to fetch a barbecue skewer to poke them out of the sky, and I caught them in my big plastic mixing bowl. They looked delightful at the far end of my table—one deep sapphire blue, the other palest blue-green—but I put them the wrong way round to begin with and didn't notice until I had dished up my dinner.

(I did think, for a moment, about digging out my extendable tape measure and trying for Pluto, but it felt unfair to include it on my table without bringing in all the other dwarf planets too, so I left it where it was.)

And so, my table decoration was complete. I stepped back to admire the colourful line of planets, sitting on my old blue table-cloth next to the plate of food, the glass of water. They were still and watchful, but even in their newfound smallness they had presence. They were giants made manageable, Titans spending the evening in my living room. When I finally sat down to eat, I felt like a god sitting down to feast on the universe.

***

When my meal was over, I pushed back my chair and looked at the food-stained plate, the crumpled napkin. Somehow the planets elevated even these; the table looked like the ruins of a bacchanalian feast, rather than the remnants of a dinner for one. But—unclaimable as they were—the planets were not mine to keep. It was time to return them to the sky.

I cleared away the dishes and brushed the crumbs off the table-cloth. Then I took hold of each corner of the cloth and pulled them together to make a bundle. The planets rolled inwards and jostled together, the great gulfs of space between them closed at last.

It took some effort to heave the bundle over the railing of my balcony, but when I finally managed it, I stood there for a few seconds, feeling the weight of the Solar System in my hands. Then I let go of two of the corners and at the same time pulled on the tablecloth so that it snapped in the air and flicked the planets skyward.

For a moment I worried they would fall. I imagined having to rush downstairs and scoop up broken planets from the car park, using shattered pieces of crust to scoop oozing mantle back inside their shells. But the planets did not fall—instead they hung in the air for a moment, shining under the summer moon, and then they tore off like comets, back to their places in the sky. After a few moments, I had lost most of them to view; only Venus hung before me, a little further along in its course than when I had pulled it out of the sky, a distant pinprick once more.

I gave the tablecloth a final shake and closed the window. My flat felt small again now, and quiet, but it was a different kind of quiet than earlier in the evening—not the scribbled silence of a worrying mind, but smooth and still, like ice. This kind of quiet—the comforting quiet of the void—could hold me for as long as I needed it to, rock me in its emptiness until there was a world, and other people's arms, to return to.

The table, now bare, was not quite clean. A few grains had fallen from the rocky planets, worked their way through the weave of the tablecloth to the wooden surface. I swept up the tiny grains— so small they almost weren't there—and held them in my hands.

Alistair Catfish

Cindy Phan

Cindy Phan writes about the everyday
fantastic, in which the boundaries
between the tragic and the absurd shift,
transform and misbehave. Her fiction
has appeared in Augur Magazine, The/
tɒmz/Review, Truancy Magazine, and
others. You can find her on Twitter: @
besidealife.

The water feature, such as it was, could only very generously, and with more than a little bit of dogged imagination, even be called such.

But it wasn't a pond and it was no longer a pool and it was hardly a fountain (though something like it, a corroded, knobbed thing, had been installed for aeration), so "water feature" it remained. Or so Colin called it as he led his dates through the semi-secluded courtyard and up the imitation wrought-iron art deco stairway to his second floor apartment.

Imitation, thought Colin with a frown. *Might have to fix that.* He bounced on his heels. *Well, why not? Tomorrow's another day. And another after that. Time enough for all things.*

Tonight, however, he had more pressing things to contend with.

The stars remained hidden, obscured by the city's harsh night-time glare, though the sky itself was clear. Had he bothered to look up, Colin might have noticed their absence.

Midnight nearly, with neighbours asleep and passersby unlikely.

The time was right. Time to make a wish. Time to call on Alistair Catfish.

As magical, wish-granting fish went, Alistair Catfish's abilities were rather underwhelming. Colin wasn't complaining, oh no. Just stating the facts, such as they were, and insofar as they related to matters concerning magical, wish-granting fish.

It's just that, if there's *magic* to be had, must it be so *limited?*

"I mean, it's kind of a tense," muttered Colin. It almost made him regret rescuing the marooned Alistair Catfish from where he found him, lying face down in the gutter after Hurricane Rina--fresh off the barely-cooled though no less ravenous heels of Hurricane Ophelia and tropical storm Philippe--made landfall and pulverized the recently-pulverized city, driving Colin away from his own water-logged abode, seeking refuge.

Almost, but not quite. Colin was no fool. He knew what he had when he found it, beat the hell up and struggling for breath, begging for salvation in exchange for a wish, or two.

"Alistair, Alistair, Alistair Catfish! Come up, come up! Come up and answer me," he said, raising his powerful, deeply resonant voice (another wish granted, thanks to Alistair Catfish) so that it drowned out the pitiable *plash-plash-plash* of the water feature.

Colin had constructed it himself out of salvaged construction materials, transforming the small pool of his duplex (yes, a *pool*, that's right, it had been a pool when all this had started) into the structure before him, filling it in with gravel and concrete to build up the sides and erode the slope from the deep end to the shallow end to the (admittedly lumpy) lip where he now stood. Waiting.

And waiting.

It had not been easy, undertaking such a backbreaking project, and all the while nursing a giant, cantankerous catfish in his bathtub. But Colin had managed it all quite well, given the circumstances. Alistair Catfish, to his credit, had even been grateful.

The stillness of the night was broken by a low gurgling, followed by a muted slap of silty water.

At last, sighed Colin.

A broad, dark snout, the colour of dried blood, mottled from where patches of dead skin clung stubbornly to it in large, tattered masses, emerged from the murky waters, glistening briefly under the white hot lights he installed around the courtyard to keep an eye on things. Colin arched a brow as water dribbled off an ungainly, lump-ridden body, watching as Alistair Catfish pushed himself laboriously into the shallows.

Here now, comes the face, mused Colin. A pair of bullwhip whiskers, unevenly tapered and heavily drooping, like wilted sunflowers that have lost their tops, dangled awkwardly in the night air, each rooted roughly on either side of a wide, racetrack of a mouth fringed with full, ever-parted lips. Colin glimpsed a pink tongue, remarkably human, and two uneven rows of teeth, thin and ragged like snapped off toothpicks. Nothing to fear there; those chompers were hardly fit for eating, let alone biting or tearing or rending--almost, in fact, something to pity, if one were so inclined.

Colin shifted his weight from one patent leather shoe to the other as two cartoonishly bugged-out eyes, planted crookedly on a boogie board of a head, gawked starkly at him.

Snout, whiskers, mouth, lips, eyes, teeth. Altogether, a quite remarkably outrageous visage. Hardly what you'd call noble, though to hear him speak, Alistair Catfish certainly thought of himself as such.

With his tail submerged and his head exposed, Alistair Catfish sucked at the air, whiskers swinging indignantly. They flapped and sagged like long wet noodles.

Huh. No preamble tonight, thought Colin peevishly. *No, I am Alistair Catfish! What is your wish?* He had come to look forward to those as part of their routine.

Well, no matter. No use calling Alistair Catfish out on his new-found reticence. Colin needed a moment to think, go over his words one last time and make sure his wish was sound.

That was, after all, the trouble with Alistair Catfish and the damnable way he granted wishes. (1) Not only were wishes *small*, they had to be *precise*: there was no wishing for grand things like wealth (what would that look like? A pile of doubloons? Six hearty and hale babies? Enlightenment, so-called?), or fame (infamy is also fame, and fame may or may not bring wealth or status and may even require destitution and/or debasement), or intelligence (such a comparative and slippery and ultimately elusive thing, genius is). That was because whatever the desired object or outcome, (2) *it had to be manifested under pre-existing conditions*--that is, it had to come from and fall within the purview of known reality. No superpowers (flying, super-strength, invisibility, etc.), or other as-yet-impossible physical manifestations or enhancements of the human form (Colin's voice almost fell into the latter category but, thanks to his teenage smoking habit and naturally deeper voice, Alistair Catfish had been able to abide him.)

(3) No violating anyone's consent, (4) NO KILLING, (5) no wishing for eternal life ("Death is in us all," crooned Alistair

Catfish), (6) no wishing beyond this particular timeline (nothing in the past or beyond the immediate future).

Otherwise, Colin was free to make as many wishes as he liked... though Alistair Catfish had initially been less than forthcoming with that last fact.

But. (7) Wish too often, and the wishes begin to lose efficacy. Buying a new car and getting free upgrades one day meant obscured concert tickets or bad ramen the next (a great pity, since there is nothing as deeply satisfying as food manifested from a simple wish).

So many rules, it made it rather tedious, all this wishing. But Colin had persevered, despite a few initial disasters (so many dreadful dinners, so many lacklustre events and disappointing trinkets). He usually got what he wanted.

He drew a deep, cleansing breath and opened his mouth to speak.

Alistair Catfish cut him off before he could utter a single, self-satisfied syllable. "You must free me! It is past due. Free me! Free me *now*, Colin Abrams!"

The audacity of this fish! Colin loathed it when Alistair Catfish called him by his full name. It was, to put it in Alistair Catfish's words, *indecorous*.

Alistair Catfish's bulging eyes roiled in his head. "This is indecorous! You must free me at once, Colin *Richard* Abrams!"

That did it. "Enough!" boomed Colin's brilliant voice. He would not lose control of the situation. Not tonight, after he finally figured out what he would wish for.

But Alistair Catfish was not so easily silenced. "I tell you true.

This cannot endure! Do not deceive yourself. I may be trapped in *this* form for *this* time, yet there is much--"

"You and your *form* owe me," Colin snapped back. "Or is your life worth so little?"

Alistair Catfish sighed heavily (the only way in which Alistair Catfish ever sighed). Large droplets of bubbling foam spilled from the corners of his mouth. "Hear me! If I were a siren, a merperson, a sovereign of the deep, you would know to take my words--"

Colin smirked. "You're not a siren or any kind of *mer* or anything close to a king, Alistair Catfish. You grant small wishes and complain. You eat my leftovers," Colin flicked his wrist as if batting away some bothersome gnats, "the occasional chihuahua. You live in a puddle." A memory of filleting bullheads with his dad came suddenly to Colin's mind.

They were in the garage. On the workbench, a wooden board with a twisted nail spiked through one end held the fish, whose heads were unceremoniously impaled on it to keep them in place.

There is not all that much to clean from the hide of a catfish--no scales or even spines to speak of (save for that wicked dorsal fin). The hide itself, however. That took work, a lot of yanking and straining with heavy pliers to rip away skin from meat. But it was worth it: battered and fried, catfish fillets were utterly delectable, though the rest of the fish was an unpalatable mess. Catching one or two would hardly do, especially for the big meals Colin's family favoured.

Colin steadied the board while his dad worked the pliers. The fish gasped and gaped.

Because he'd asked, his dad showed him that, *yes a decapitated catfish still moved*, still flailed its body and flapped its mouth, as if still breathing, as if still alive.

"Stupid thing," Colin's father scoffed with a measure of pity and more than a little disgust. "Why don't you die?" He picked up the head and tossed the quivering mass into the garbage.

Colin bent low as if indeed addressing a king. "If I cut off your head, Alistair Catfish, would you still roll your eyes? Would you still gasp for breath?" he sneered. "Would it be worth denying me then?"

Alistair Catfish ceased his admonitions.

Moths clouded the flat white lights. The foetid waters surrounding them seethed, as if in a slow boil.

"I am Alistair Catfish," Alistair Catfish finally whispered.

Colin drew himself up to his full height. "Of course you are." He straightened his tie. He cleared his throat, fidgeting with his custom-made cufflinks, suddenly self-conscious now that the moment was upon them. "So. There is a woman."

Alistair Catfish smacked his lips in disdain. "Hm! Apartment 2. You are cruel but *typical*, Colin Abrams."

"And you will do as I wish."

"I will do as you wish," Alistair Catfish answered after a beat.

Colin caught his reflection, a wash-out head that had appeared behind the spot where Alister Catfish flopped his tail. His wavy blonde hair was perfectly in place. His nose pointed, prim and proud; his own lips a thin, resolute line. Only his eyes, made an unnatural glowing blue against the vile brown-grey slosh of the water, betrayed his nervousness.

"Mail," he said, with a rushed finality, as if ordering randomly off an overpriced menu. "Starting tomorrow, and for a whole week, I wish that all the mail from Apartment 2 of this house be sent to my mailbox instead." He snapped his fingers, done with the matter, daring Alistair Catfish to disobey him.

The lights above them flickered. Moths teemed around the glass.

Alistair Catfish lunged, bringing himself within inches of where Colin stood, and snapped his cavernous maw, missing some rather crucial anatomy of Colin's by a few precious degrees. Colin, too surprised to flinch or cry out, remained frozen in rigid disbelief.

"I am Alistair Catfish! Your wish is granted," snarled Alistair Catfish, falling back into the muck. Duty fulfilled, hurled himself back into the darkness of the water, soaking Colin's shoes in brackish sludge as he went.

***

Three quick knocks brought her to the door.

Colin flashed her a dazzling smile. "Brooke? I'm Colin. Colin Abrams. I live upstairs. Welcome to the house! And," he rushed on, "I don't mean to disturb you, but I've got some of your mail." He handed her the flyers, McDonald's coupons, and subscription to *Hello! Magazine* that had arrived for her during the past seven days.

"Two can dine for $11.98! Isn't that something?" she said, reading the coupons. "A shame it doesn't rhyme. 'Ninety-nine' and it would really sing." When she looked up at Colin he found that he wholeheartedly agreed.

Brooke Trinh of Apartment 2, her mail read. She was taller than most women, but at her full height only reached Colin's chin so it was okay. Her jet black hair shone a dark, lustrous brown in the sun, which set off her rich olive skin quite prettily. She wore a pair of designer frames--thick, square, and blood-red--which curiously hid her features (the hazel of her eyes, the shape of her nose, and the set of her mouth) unless you *really* looked.

She had captivated Colin so completely he thought of little else, even his increasingly ill-gotten wishes. She had moved in at the end of the month, after that irksome Mr. Fitzpatrick finally vacated the premises, panicked that another one of his precious little show dogs would disappear.

Brooke smiled warmly at Colin from behind her impressive frames. "Colin. Colin Abrams. You're the landlord?" Her voice had a slight lilt to it, an accent he wasn't expecting and couldn't quite place.

"Only in an official capacity," chuckled Colin. "The building manager, Andy, he runs the day-to-day stuff around this place. Actually helped my parents split this big old house in two after they bought it. He's good, but not around very often. Our place isn't the only building under his care." *Was he babbling?*

(He was babbling.)

Brooke nodded. "Andy, yes. He showed me the apartment. Nice man. Pisces." She winked.

Colin couldn't help himself. He leaned against the doorframe and cocked his head. "And what's *your* sign?" he said with a roguish grin.

And here Brooke's eyes went wide and she laughed. Laughed and laughed, sweetly and delicately, like a half-remembered lullaby, music to Colin's ears.

***

"It's this a new railing? It looks different. Stylish. Classy. It really suits, the uh...it really suits the place..." Brooke's voice trailed off.

"Oh, this old thing?" answered Colin absently, hurrying on ahead. "I can't wait for you to see my place!"

"What *is* that?" Brooke descended the staircase, striking each step with the chic platforms of her high-heeled shoes.

"Brooke? Honey? Where are you going?" Colin cried out, alarmed.

By the time he caught up with her, Brooke was standing by the deep end of the water feature. "Something's in there...It's a fish! Oh, Colin, why didn't you tell me there were *fish* in here?" She smiled.

Because Alistair Catfish is supposed to stay out of sight, as per our arrangement. Because I just can't wish *him away, can I?* thought Colin bitterly. *Because* who cares *about fish?*

The water rippled and swelled. As Colin scrambled to say something about surreptitious koi, Alistair Catfish surfaced, maneuvering his great bulk so that first his head then his tail grazed the surface of the water.

When he rose again, Colin was nearly apoplectic with anger and more than a little undercut by fear. While Brooke *oooed* and *ahhed*, marveling at the wonderous creature before her, he shot Alistair Catfish a murderous glance.

Don't do it. Don't you do it, Alistair Catfish!

"I am Alistair Catfish!" proclaimed Alistair Catfish. He splashed and leapt, spun and dove, showing off.

"Oh. My. God," squealed Brooke. "Ohmygod, OHMYGOD!"

Colin had the presence of mind to grab her before she lost her balance and toppled headlong into the rank water.

***

Love is a strange thing, and rather absurd. When Colin was with Brooke, he found his mind sometimes wandered--she had a tendency to simply delight in every little thing, from bluebirds to telephone booths to root vegetables to barbed wire, and it was kind of a lot. Yet, when he was without her, he thought of nothing else but being with her again, of needing to keep her at his side, whatever the cost.

It didn't help, her new-found obsession with Alistair Catfish. *He* was all they talked about anymore. He dominated every conversation, every word, except maybe, 'hello,' and 'goodbye,' and even then, unless they were alone together, Colin wasn't always sure if Brooke was addressing him or *him*.

It was, therefore, a small mercy that beyond his proclamations of 'I am Alistair Catfish'! Alistair Catfish said little else to Brooke.

Of course, such mercy came at a price: better grub (in this case, literally, and Colin now found himself running quite an exorbitant tab at a nearby bait shop as well as an account at Salvador's Meats that was actually mind boggling), cleaner waters (which also took much of Colin's time and even more of his money for filtration equipment, bacteria treatments, and purification tablets), and extra time between wishes, "to rest, to replenish," said Alistair Catfish, and "because your greed must be ebbed, one way or another, Colin *Richard* Abrams."

After all, for Brooke, the thrill of Alistair Catfish was not just in the incredible fact and unassailable veracity of him, but also in the idea that she and Colin were the only two people to know it. The woman, it seemed, loved her secrets. Of things remaining that way, Colin had little doubt: Brooke was the first person he'd ever dated that didn't have an Insta account, wasn't on Twitter, and was totally ignorant regarding all things Facebook. She rarely texted or answered her phone, assuming that she had it with her in the first place, which was seldom.

The more he thought about it, the more he realized that there wasn't all that much he knew about Brooke Trinh beyond what little she told him. Something about possibly being descended from royalty (but then, she laughed, who wasn't?). Something about a river and a city square. But what else? Family? Friends? He wasn't even sure he knew where she worked, despite being of all things, her landlord.

But now he knew how he would find out.

"Alistair, Alistair, Alistair Catfish! Come up, come up! Come up and answer me," Colin sang to a catchy little tune he wrote himself. That had been his latest wish: to understand sheet music so that he could not only sing--a wish he'd made a few days previous, realizing that while his voice had become divine, he himself had been a little tone-deaf--but compose. The notes and annotations always seemed a jumble to Colin. Now, he read them with ease.

He wrote Brooke a song ("Lovely She Runs"). Brooke, while duly impressed, had suggested that he ought to write a ballad about Alistair Catfish.

Colin had suppressed a scowl at that. But the song (*Alistair, Alistair, Alistair Catfish... Alistair, Alistair, Alistair Catfish!*) had already begun to take shape in his mind. He let the melody wash over him, saw the notes take shape and form, as easy and natural as breathing.

And that's when he knew he had it: a way not around but *through* Alistair Catfish's godforsaken *rules.*

"Such a splendid fellow! Such a remarkable fish! He'd make a wonderful song," Brooke continued, as Colin stood there, gripped in the throes of epiphany. She reclined on a beach chair she set up in the courtyard, sunbathing while Alistair Catfish basked in the shallows, dorsal fin piercing the sky. "Is that the water purification stuff? Pass it here so I can add it to the water."

Colin numbly handed Brooke the bag containing the tablets.

Alistair Catfish spared him a smug glance as if to say, *Keep your love, why don't you?*

Tonight Colin would do precisely that.

He watched as the enormous face crested the water, nearly jumped back as Alistair Catfish launched himself so far forward it seemed as if he were planning to simply overtake the shallows and keep right on going into the courtyard, as if that, too, had become his domain. The thought rankled Colin, perhaps more than it should.

Perhaps one day he'd become a less petty man, or at least wish to be one.

"I am Alistair Catfish!" beamed Alistair Catfish, looking positively radiant. The dead patches of skin were gone, his eyes were a cool, liquid black and his whiskers jutted from his face fiercely, as if ready for battle.

Alistair Catfish swished his tail so that it fanned out in the shallows, a gossamer sail adrift in dark waters. "Colin Abrams! Where has the Lady gone?"

Colin's expression soured. "What business is that of yours?" Though it wasn't like Colin exactly knew. Brooke said she would be busy tonight and neglected to elaborate.

Alistair Catfish actually smiled. "I enjoy being in the company of the Lady!"

Good for you, Colin thought bitterly.

And then he too smiled, wide and true.

***

In the end, it was, as all the others had been, a small wish. Nothing earth-shattering or life-changing in the grandest sense, except, perhaps, for poor Alistair Catfish.

"I've realized something," Colin went on as Alistair Catfish eyed him warily, not liking his captor's new-found confidence. "I didn't start out with this magnificent voice. And I couldn't sing with it until, thanks to you, I could. And now, I can compose. I can *see* and *feel* the music where before there was nothing."

"Hm!" replied Alistair Catfish crossly, at a loss, at last, for words.

Colin began pacing slowly, savouring the moment. "Don't you see? Ever since I met you, Alistair Catfish, the bounds of my reality have shifted. Bit by bit and slowly, very slowly. But shifting all the same."

Alistair Catfish gnashed his teeth, but said nothing.

Colin approached the water's edge and stared down at Alistair Catfish. "So many wishes. And it's not like you ever *really* said no. Even with all those rules, all those caveats and *restrictions*, in the end, you can't say no, not a definite one, can you? One way or another, I get what I want," he declared, with a rightness that he felt deep in his bones.

Alistair Catfish withdrew into the water until it reached his gills. Colin watched as it rippled, disturbed by the trembling fury that overtook Alistair Catfish. Finally, after much effort, he stilled and glared wrathfully at Colin.

"No," conceded Alistair Catfish. "No, I cannot."

"I knew it!" shouted Colin, triumphant. "I knew it!" The possibilities whirled inside his head. So there was indeed so much more to it, all this wishing, and he intended to make good use of it, rewrite the rules and finally, truly avail himself to his heart's content, the world, and Alistair Catfish, be damned.

"I fucking knew it!" he whooped.

Yes, he would break Alistair Catfish, one wish at a time.

But first.

"I wish for you to banish yourself to the depths of these waters, unable to swim up to the surface unless I allow it!" Colin would tell Brooke that Alistair Catfish had become sullen (perhaps because he was ill or because, honestly, this type of thing happened from time to time with Alistair Catfish). He'd begin to experiment, using wishes at varying intervals (every five days, four, three and so on) to test their efficacy, see if a free movie one day would allow for a chance encounter with a celebrity (however minor) the next. He'd take Brooke to the best restaurants, the coolest hot-spots, impress her with trips to cottage country and weekend getaways to sandy white beaches.

In time, he'd wish away her fascination with Alistair Catfish, even her memory of him if he could manage it. After that, wealth, fame, power...Hell, he'd keep going until he took the moon itself, until Alistair Catfish was reduced to a withered carcass of fishy flesh and spent indignation.

Colin narrowed his eyes, daring Alistair Catfish to challenge him. "Well?"

"I am Alistair Catfish," wailed Alistair Catfish. "Your wish is granted."

***

Brooke's concern over Alistair Catfish, while infuriating at first, eventually abated until all Colin really had to contend with were comparatively light inquiries over whether Alistair Catfish had resurfaced. He reassured her with lies, distracted her with big romantic gestures.

It was all so remarkably easy, and it was for the best.

"I saw him the other night after you went to bed. He seems good. Ornery, but good," said Colin, fraying his voice just so--testimony to the enduring fact that everything was okay.

Brooke shook her head as if to break his spell. "Oh, Colin. Was it something I did?"

"No, honey, no! He'll come around." Colin put his arm around her shoulders. Soothed, she kissed him lightly on his lips.

There had been little time, with all the wining and dining and traveling they did, for Colin to truly set his plans in motion for ultimate wish fulfillment, but what, after all, was the rush?

Granted, even he knew he would soon grow bored of the fleeting glamours of his current lifestyle. But not yet.

And if Brooke had any reservations about attention he lavished on her, it never once showed in anything she said or did. In fact, she had *insisted* on the trips after Colin suggested they go away together, made so many of her own suggestions on *the* best places to go that he eventually let her choose their destinations.

Which was why the note he found proved particularly devastating.

Colin, oh how I would have loved to devour you myself.

XXX,

B.

He found it under his door, sealed in an aquamarine envelope. It had come the day after he finally managed to return home from a disastrous glass-bottom boat tour Brooke got him to book online ("I know it's mostly dying coral and half-starved sea life, but it'll be worth it," Brooke had said, and who was he to argue with that?).

Yet, before they could set their eyes on a single outcropping of belched-out reef, an unexpected (as in unseasonal, as in *monstrous*) tempest descended upon their vessel, tossing it in the churning waters so violently it seemed certain it would shatter and they would drown. Passengers screamed and wept and made bargains with their assorted gods; children rolled down aisles; parents were pitched out of their seats; couples banged up against each other.

All the while, Colin held on tight to Brooke, who remained so silent and serene throughout the whole ordeal, it was clear that she had gone into some terrible shock.

It was only by some miracle they made it back to shore, during an abrupt lull in the storm. As they disembarked, Colin leading Brooke by the shoulders, it picked up again, washing out roads, drowning cattle, whipping all manner of things from the sea (buoys, skiffs, discombobulated octopi), and stranding everyone, absolutely everyone, tourists and locals alike, for days on end in a dinky little town whose name Colin had trouble even remembering.

But even before the sky had cleared and the sea quieted at last, he woke up to find her gone.

She did not return his calls.

He did not have her email.

She did not text him back.

Had they been in love?

They'd been in love!

He had loved her. He was sure of it.

Colin's first impulse had been to bang on the door of Apartment 2 to demand an explanation from the wayward Brooke. No answer, and by the stillness of the air inside and heavy silence behind the door, it was clear that there hadn't been anyone home for quite some time. Colin went behind the house and into the courtyard. He fixed his gaze on the water feature. No signs of life there, either, save for the bubbles that raised languidly to the surface and then burst oozing like large, fat cysts.

For a long time, he remained there, lost in thought. In the end, exhausted and weary, and unsure of what, exactly, he wanted in that moment--what wish could possibly wash away his bitterness or soothe his heartache?--he retreated to the comfort of his suite.

Alistair Catfish could wait.

***

Was it a risk calling on Alistair Catfish so early in the day? Perhaps, but then there may have been a part of Colin seeking the kind of validation that comes with getting caught in the act. Something for him to show off, in his own way, finally.

"Alistair, Alistair, Alistair Catfish! Come up, come up! Come up and answer me!" Colin waited, astonished at how good it felt, getting back into a routine. Reclaiming himself.

And so he waited.

And waited.

The knob atop the water feature burbled and spat.

Nothing--not a splash or a sputter from Alistair Catfish. Colin raked the shallows with anxious eyes. The water seemed even more solid than usual, like an ice sheet formed in the dead of winter, and closed off in a way that shamed him for looking.

Panicked now, he tried again. "Alistair, Alistair, Alistair Catfish!"

Nothing.

Colin paced the courtyard in long, desperate strides. "Alistair, Alistair, Alistair Catfish...!"

There was a disturbance in the leaflitter that fringed the water feature. He crouched down to investigate. *Tracks?* Raccoon.

Or possum, maybe. Something with stretched-out palms and tapered fingers (something Colin might have even conceded was closer to that of a lost child or escaped chimpanzee had he the wherewithal). There was a smell, mossy and sour-sweet, that he could not place. It wafted around him, hinting at something; a lurking menace.

He ran to Andy's storage shed, grabbed a long shovel and stabbed into the water, probing, searching, hoping against hope...and more than a little frightened about what he might find.

"Where are you? Where are you, Alistair Catfish? *Show yourself!*"

Nothing but that insolent silence. Nothing but Alistair Catfish's astounding absence.

For hours Colin searched, threatened, cajoled, and for his efforts was rewarded only with soiled clothes, a sore throat, and an aching back.

Can cat fish drown? Could Alistair Catfish? Could he really die after all?

In the morning, he would drain the water feature, rip up the tiles and dig under the mud--with his bare hands if it came to it---so he could be sure.

He had to be sure.

***

Sleep would not come. Neither would the sweet release of drunken stupor. And there Colin was out of ideas.

He lay in bed fully dressed, reeking of the afternoon's efforts.

Crushed beer cans were scattered across the polished hardwood floor.

"Alistair, Alistair, Alistair Catfish...where have you gone?" Colin smacked his lips, much like he'd seen Alistair Catfish so many times before.

Head throbbing, he opened his mouth to truly rile against the torments that had befell him.

He heard it. A dull, wet slap against the windowpane--a thunking like an open meaty palm smacking a cellophane-wrapped coconut.

Colin ceased his lamentations. He heard it again, but closer, somewhere in the vicinity of his front foyer, against the windows of the living room.

There came a creaking, the sound of an unlocked door being pushed open, then a scuttling, a *patter-patter-patter* of moist, soft steps.

Colin swallowed hard, resisted the urge to pull the blankets over his head.

Patter-patter-patter. Pitter-patter-patter.

Something was in the room. Colin willed himself silent. A sharp chill prickled his spine. He squeezed his eyes shut.

No. Not just in the room but, as the mattress sagged and his sheets were soaked through, *in his bed.*

"Colin Abrams," it whispered from the foot of his bed. "Colin Richard Abrams!" it roared.

White spots danced across his field of vision as the wind was knocked out of him and Colin's eyes shot open. His limbs flailed uselessly and then were roughly pinned down. He realized with horror that his body had been immobilized by four flat, wriggling things--two on his chest and arms, two crushing his thighs as if they were loaves of fresh bread.

"I AM ALISTAIR CATFISH!" howled Alistair Catfish, a war cry that slammed into Colin and shook the walls of his apartment. Alistair Catfish howled again. Howled and *stomped*, sending shockwaves of pain through Colin's torso, whipping him once, twice and again (and then once more, for good measure) with those wickedly sharp, barbed whiskers.

Feet, Colin realized with sudden, crystal clear revulsion. They were *feet*. Smooth, elongated catfish feet and...*toes?* Gnarled, large-knuckled, finger-like toes.

An ugly thought raced through Colin's mind. *Did the first fish to walk on land have six little toes, each fitted with its own thickened, yellow toenail?*

His stomach clenched. Bile burned the inside of his mouth.

Alistair Catfish loomed over him. For the second time since Colin first knew him, Alistair Catfish smiled, lighting up his face in all its heinous glory.

"I am Alistair Catfish!" he bellowed once more. "What is your wish?"

Colin's neurons fired in all directions, frantically seeking an escape. "I wish you were dead!" he cried out, hysterical, no longer caring about anything but his own immediate survival.

(Ah, but Alistair Catfish lived only in the moment.)

Alistair Catfish erupted in laughter. His belly shook and sloshed until he belched, spewing partially-digested house pets, wet and reeking--the fastidious part of Colin's mind clocked a half-chewed parakeet, an iguana head, and an entire miniature dachshund--onto his 1,000 thread count Egyptian cotton sheets.

Alistair Catfish licked his chops. "Another wish perhaps, Colin Abrams?"

Teeth chattering, heart banging so hard he felt it in his bowels, Colin tried again. "I-I-I wish for you to go back to the pool!" he stammered.

(Ah, but it was no longer a pool, was it? And what, exactly, was a "water feature" anyway?).

Alistair Catfish flicked his foot. A toenail struck Colin in the face, slicing the inside of his nostril, drawing blood.

"Pitiful! And from one so clever. Shall I help you, Colin Abrams?" mocked Alistair Catfish. "Do you wish me to wish your wish?"

Twisting his body to one side, Colin freed an arm and swung at Alistair Catfish, landing a soft blow against his massive underside.

Alistair Catfish barely flinched.

"I wish...I wish for you to go away! LEAVE ME ALONE!" Colin screamed as he punched, hot tears streaking his face.

(Ah, but Alistair Catfish would leave only in his own due time.)

Which wishes, which wishes, which wishes from which? To grant? Temper? Ignore? Only Alistair Catfish knew for sure. Only Alistair Catfish could tell which wish from which.

Only someone like Colin would presume otherwise.

Colin's mind reeled as it grappled with his current, inordinately uncontrivable reality. Had all that trembling flesh that formed Alistair Catfish's body actually been unyielding muscle? Had Alistair Catfish always been man-sized? Larger, in fact, than life itself?

Had he always dwarfed Colin so?

No! Yes! thought Colin as Alistair Catfish leaned in hard with his horrible catfish feet.

He's the same as he's ever been. He's the same as he ever was.

"Not a king, but a Catfish, Colin Abrams. If only you listened." Alistair Catfish opened his prodigious mouth, revealing manifold rows of sharp, pointed teeth.

Stalactite and stalagmites of pain, thought Colin stupidly.

As the darkness claimed him, Colin realized that all the wishes in the world wouldn't have saved him, even if he'd had all the time in that world to wish them.

The power of his wishes had always been beyond him. Time, as he knew it, was a trifling concept, and a rather senseless endeavour, compared to that.

Little by little and yet all at once, things change. And change again. How could it be otherwise? Otherwise was death itself.

He was almost grateful, if only for that last, final insight.

***

The dreadful white lights had been extinguished for good. Nast preferred the shadows. She stood barefoot in the courtyard, those lovely but oh-so-painful (but still *very* lovely) heels abandoned inside Apartment 2 along with a few other things she'd picked up during her sojourn.

She sighed. For all its flaws, she would miss this place, all that dirt under her feet, all those rocks, acorns, and small bones she collected just because she enjoyed them so.

She would, however, keep the frames. If merfolk could horde forks and lovers surely she could keep one pair of glasses. See if anybody had anything to say about that!

By her side stood the one and only Alistair Catfish.

Nast smiled. "You gave us quite a scare, Alistair Catfish. Even my father expressed his concern, in his own way."

Alistair Catfish looked up at her in wonderment. "Is that so?"

"He asked, ostensibly in passing, if I had seen you," Nast quickly amended so as not to lead Alistair Catfish too far astray. She shrugged, weary, as always, of her taciturn father and his intractable pride. "Of course, by then *I* could no longer bear your absence and was on my way to find you. Kraken, indeed, was especially worried, and bid me make haste," she added, knowing Alistair Catfish would love to hear it.

"Hm! They will rise soon enough," Alistair Catfish answered sagaciously, pleased. Be it deep-sea leviathans, the Great Sea King himself (in his own way), or resourceful nymphs like her, all admired (or perhaps better yet, owed some debt to) Alistair Catfish.

Nast frowned. "Did you not sense the storm coming, Alistair Catfish? Did you not feel it?"

"It was like nothing I have ever experienced before," confessed Alistair Catfish. "I was ripped from the river and blown clear across the accused sky before I even knew it!" He sighed. "The world is changing, Nast. Hot, poisoned, capricious. Hardly fit for humans, let alone gods, large or small. "

"Oh? Do you fancy yourself a *god*, Alistair Catfish?" teased Nast.

"Well," replied Alistair Catfish, not meeting her eye. "I *could* be. Not a large one. But, not a small one either."

Nast pondered that a moment. "You could have given him so much more. Even, I suspect, everything." The smile was back. "All those rules!"

Alistair Catfish smacked his lips. His whiskers buzzed. "I merely waxed philosophical, proposing what *might* be so, insinuated how to wish *proper* wishes, given the...hm! Given the circumstances," he finished in a huff.

Can catfish blush? thought Nast as Alistair Catfish turned away from her, pretending to snap his teeth at non-existent prey, a dragonfly or hummingbird, perhaps. She indulged him his indiscretion. They both knew the cesspool that had been his prison had nothing remotely filling, let alone nourishing, to offer, despite its recent cleansing. Perhaps if Colin Abrams had provided more potable waters there would have been more weight behind his wishes, more gravitas, at least, until Alistair Catfish recuperated and freed himself.

Nast knew Alistair Catfish was remembering finer days, pristine waters in which he swelled enormous. She too longed for days gone past, when people came to her waters, offering gifts in exchange for the small tidings she had within her own power to give them.

No more. At least, not right now, and not anytime that could even remotely be conceived of in human terms as "soon," if indeed there were any humans left when the world took its next turn into another era.

"'Yea, foolish mortals,'" she said softly so that it drifted away into the hot summer's night. "'Noah's flood is not yet subsided; two thirds of the fair world it yet covers.'" She shook her head. "And yet they continue on, proclaiming the world inexhaustible, convinced that it is theirs alone, and that in any case they will survive it, despite themselves. Such grand presumptions, are they not?"

"Melville or," and here Alistair Catfish affected a mocking tone, "*man*?" And then Alistair Catfish really did laugh. But only for a moment. He became sombre, his countenance marked by trepidation. "And Great Nast, do you also find *me* foolish? I confess I...I do not know what would have become of me had you not intervened."

Nast did not hesitate. "You are Alistair Catfish. You are miraculous. Miraculous and irrefutable." She reached for him and kissed him soundly on his catfish mouth.

"Welll!" exclaimed Alistair Catfish.

Oh yes, catfish do indeed blush. Nast laughed, releasing him. "Did you devour him then?" Her eyes sparkled at the very idea of it. Mortals amused her in so very many ways. How she *adored* them.

Alistair Catfish demurred. "They are, as you say, foolish. But they are also unfailingly *mortal*. It seemed more than he deserved, such a fate as that."

"So then, Alistair Catfish, what have you done to our own foolish, mortal man?"

Alistair Catfish flexed his toes. The sensation was exquisite. "Look upon the water, Nast, and see for yourself."

Between the shallows and the deep, Nast spotted it: a bulbous head, and huge, compared to the slip of a body attached to it, as if by mistake, or at best, afterthought.

"Ah," said Nast, taking in the poor, unfortunate soul. "And now?"

Alistair Catfish clicked his tongue. "Perhaps a prince or princess will find him and bestow upon him a gift--a kiss for redemption, or a plate for deliverance. Perhaps his gills will fail as these waters rot and he along with them. Perhaps the rains will wash away the decay and he will, at last, find himself. It is no concern of ours, Nast. *We* will go on, as ever, or as best *we* can." With that, Alistair Catfish turned his back from the water feature, never to offend his eyes again with the sight of it.

After a brief prayer, Nast followed him.

Two mournful cerulean eyes watched them as they disappeared. The head bobbed listlessly back and forth like something cheap and possibly flimsy.

If it heard any of the things said about its fate, it didn't have a word to say anything about it.

Thin Crust

Erin MacNair

Erin MacNair is a short story writer from North Vancouver, Canada.

First appeared in The Walrus magazine, March of 2017

The fisherman only got a quick glimpse. Normally the morning light that burst forth from the waves was a panacea; it made fumbling in darkness into a cold boat reeking of dried fish slime worth it. Today, however, something was amiss. It made him fearful. He crooked his neck to check the shoreline of Los Cabos, its jagged teeth just visible. He turned back to watch the horizon line as it wavered unevenly, then set as if stone. It was close, this instant wall, a frozen indigo roadblock spanning as far as he could see. The man looked upwards, squinting, bothered by the shifting umber insistence that all was normal; the sun was coming up just as it always had. There was quiet, too much of it, an unnatural end to the sea's voice. The man felt this non-noise in his stomach as a dull pain before his head rendered meaning. A cormorant flew past, dipped into the waves; missed its catch. It flew on, black body flapping towards the demarcation, where it slipped silently into nothing. There. Not there. The Fisherman blinked as if willing the vision to dislodge. Soon the fish followed. First, only a few flung their bodies over this horizontal partition, slices of wet muscle absorbed into space. Then a shoal of silvery herring, vomiting themselves into the abyss, soaring between where the sky should be and where the Ocean should have welcomed them into another breath.

The man began to pray. What else was he to do?

"Ave Maria llena eres de gracia..."

He listened now, sharpening all attention to what might be. The remaining waves moved his small boat towards the fleeing fish, the invisible bird. They lapped at the fiberglass, a sound he'd always loved, little warm blankets of noise. He continued to pray and dropped the oars, instead focusing on the back of his hands, hands hewn by fishing hooks and weathering salt and high levels of sun. They shook momentarily.

The seafarers saw it first. They did not have the words to relay what they were seeing. How could one describe there were *edges* to the Ocean? There was now a place to fall from? This could not be possible. Nor could it be possible that the waves no longer rose and fell. They had died, left behind a hazy mirror. The sky was impossibly still, wispy clouds replaced by cumulus, fat sheep lazing in the blue. As far as anyone knew time was still passing, clocks were still working. They were all still breathing, speaking, no? There was a camaraderie, a brotherhood, on the ships. We are in this together, we are seeing this together. Can we confirm what this is? Was it a continental shift, a new drop off? Was this smear of oblivion some trickery of the light? They picked up headsets and radios; tried to explain, until they would see a ship in front of them dissolve into nothing. Then they would drop the handsets and try in vain to turn around, no longer thrilled with the prospect of learning something new before anyone else. On land the messages were garbled, confusing. Slavic, Icelandic, and Asiatic voices burst forth from the airwaves, straining to be heard, like marbles swirling at the bottom of a barrel. *The sea has an end. We are falling off the edge of the earth.* Or just, *Aggghhhhhhh!!* This caused alarm, but not as much as the fact that cell phone coverage was now spotty at best.

The masses were annoyed. What was wrong with the satellites?

Millions of swears lifted into the air, a salty brine of languages dipped in confusion and anger. *What the hell. Is. Wrong?*

WE'RE SORRY, YOUR SERVICE HAS BEEN TEMPORARILY INTERRUPTED.

No explanation, nothing. This was an outrage. Who did this? Was this ISIS? Were they under attack? Did the tower down the street just fritz out? That was not supposed to happen. They paid a lot for this service, you know. Things like this were *not supposed to happen*, not for more than three minutes at a time. People bumped into each other on the sidewalks, checking and re-checking, checking again. They held their hands up, hoping for a signal. The fact that everyone was having a problem did not bode well. Not *all* of them could have missed their payments, however impossibly high they were for such simple tasks as texting and endless perusal of Facebook. They held their devices like dying animals they had devoted their lives to. Please. Please work. My life is on here.

The first person one should call would be the scientist. They did, all the important people anyway. He answered the phone diligently for about an hour, at which point he got sick of saying *I don't know anything yet* so pinched out the cord from the back of the phone. *Think man.* He'd presented his thesis to the board six months ago, written it up. *Scientific American* had done a piece on it. Everyone agreed it had gone well, even though it couldn't be proved. Dark Matter was one of those things, it might not even exist. Einstein thought it did, so everyone else thought the possibility was there too. His mother had liked the article, although she hadn't understood most of it. He thought this might have been the case with many. They nodded in the right places and asked a few questions but really it had flown right over them, thought bubbles bursting into droplets of stale air. The scientist scratched at his beard, which he had grown during an ironic bet but later began to like. He looked like a dapper young homeless man, in his thin coat and scruffy face. It suited him. Made people stare into his blue eyes, avoiding a good look at his unkempt accoutrement. It threw them off, which he found useful. He didn't like to be packaged. He'd done that himself, and now he was without a family, a hobby, a habit. He was a man consumed. This might prove itself to be a good thing. Perhaps it was meant to be, this consumption. He could give back, make it all worth it. He checked the Hubble, thankfully still in contact, and began typing $v = HoD$ into the keyboard. The Scientist added more numbers, then plugged the phone back in. He made a call to a seismologist, a friend. He confirmed, they too had been doing some testing. The friend asked *had he heard about Utah?* No, he had not. *No time for Utah*, the friend said. *The Earth is only two miles down.* What, the scientist said. *You heard me*, the friend said. The scientist hung up the phone. The Earth was flat.

Bryce Canyon was as beautiful as Utah could get, and the couple were going all the way up to Rainbow Ridge. With a name like that, something good was bound to happen, some spark could be lit. The couple were happy. At least, they told themselves they were fairly happy, and the more recent painful events were just a momentary blip on the relationship scale. They would go and see some natural beauty like they used to when they had been more romantically inclined. She had recently found religion. He had not. This was only one of the sticking points. They were going to shelve it for this early morning hike, and they were first in the park, first to drive to the very top. Parking off the beaten path, they hiked up, holding hands. She thought this might be forcing it, he was trying too hard, and it impaired her maneuvering of the trail. But she liked the warmth and roughness of his working hand holding her manicured one. They could do this. Everything would be alright. The couple burst through the last few trees and exhaled, stunned by the beauty before them. The amphitheater of golden red rock was eerie beauty: swaths of ochre, strokes of fir green. The Park pamphlet had said *breathtaking* and *magnificent* and he immediately felt those were inadequate platitudes. He turned his head to tell her, pausing to consider small wisps of hair dancing around the edges of her shoulders. She was still so very beautiful. He meant to say this, but paused, puzzled. She frowned, her face crumpling inwards as she pointed one lanky finger forward. Their personal viewfinder was burning up at the edges. The scene before them eroded, like the aluminum in an Etch-A-Sketch, shaken by the almighty. This is what she thought anyway.

God is loosening his hold. God is planning something for me, at this moment. I knew it. I knew it.

He just thought *What the fuck?!*

It was now an empty blackness, past their rocky perch. The sun still shone behind them, casting a glow over the shimmering nothingness. She made as if to touch it and he shouted at her, alarmed. She turned and smiled at him, and then pitched herself in.

A flint-spark, then a cold space. Tiny flecks of light all around her. The cold was momentary, replaced with an awareness that she shared molecules with every one of these stars. She'd known this, heard it in the messages: she was one of Gods' special spirit children. One day they would rise into his realm, first. She was chosen for this. These thoughts peeled away as conscious thought departed, replaced with a practical freedom that involved nothing of one's previous patterns. There was light, there was motion, there was a community of cells that fit together, and all previous confines gave way to a subtle warmth, an arching beam. She was consumed by something larger.

The scientist focused on his computer now, sifting through the options in his head, prioritizing them in a matter of seconds. He punched his fingers into the keyboard and pulled up the Hubble view. The picture was fading already, reaching the outskirts. It blinked into darkness, a shifting inkiness, like a wet towel had been thrown over the telescopic eye. It strained for light, finding tiny bits. He scrutinized the screen, but there was nothing there. He was imagining the light, if there was any. He must be. Surly this was what he'd known could happen, if the expansion of space could accelerate...hadn't it all been in the article? The discrepancy in measurements, the acoustic oscillatory data collected from near and distant galaxies? It could happen. It was very unlikely to only consume half of a planet, but hey, this was really quite unknown stuff here. Who's to say, really. Odd, for sure. But a definite maybe. The math didn't support it, but it had never occurred to anyone to apply it this way, so, yeah. The scientist linked his tower signal to his computer. If anyone was listening, he would let them know what he thought. He keyed in his most powerful telescope and directed it into the void.

The masses were taking it in now, the seriousness of it. News from around the world showed shot after shot of the anti-matter, until the satellites blinked out. Children were sent outside to play and told not to worry. They did worry but kept themselves occupied until they were allowed to know more. The west coast of North America was seemingly gone; with it any real estate hierarchy. A few had discerned that the Edge bisected the Earth neatly, cleaved it right in two. That was the rumour, and it spread. If family was close, they went to them, offered their sweating bodies and worried frowns to each other as comfort. If family was in China, Australia, Japan, most of Russia, places like Indonesia and Alaska, well, there was no hope.

There wasn't the panic one might expect. It was as if this Edge, this Dark exuded a calm peace, a vibrational healing. Of course, this didn't work on everybody (just like some are repulsed by the smell of lavender). A few ran about with home made signs of doom, shouted from the tops of courtyard spaces. Some smashed windows and made to take things, but then realized there wasn't much point to that after all, if they couldn't even get Netflix. The ones with guns and ammunition were quite vindicated and felt this was the moment they had planned for all along, why hadn't anyone listened to them. But after hunkering down in safe-houses and bunkers they too, forgot what really the point of it all was. Maybe they should just talk with each other for awhile. Just, speak of things. And this is what they did. They laid hands on shoulders and talked of ideas they thought important, things that were beauty incarnate and what was the craziest thing that ever happened to them? Some traveled to remote places to be with those who had no family. Those in the remotest of locations stayed there, happy to be away from others, somewhat oblivious to the whole hoo-ha except for the feeling of peace. *It was a nice day on the mountain,* they thought, and just went about things.

The scientist spoke into his computer, staring into it with his best stern/serious face.

...and I have been proposing this scenario for years, this kind of thing could happen at any time, really. We are at the mercy of the forces of nature. I do not think this is the time to panic, however, this is the time for the world to come together. To build our new future...

He had always wanted to give a speech like this. An important one, where he would be recognized as a leader, a mind of great expansiveness, a person of authority.

The scientist realized he had paused and should continue to pull out as many words of substance as he could muster.

...a future in which we pool our resources, support the remaining population with innovation...

A blip on the screen next to him. The scientist remembered to excuse himself.

...One moment...

He turned his full attention to the telescopic screen. There was something in the darkness. At first, he opened his eyes widely, blinking away any haziness. No, there was something. Not just a blip or an eye fuzz. He moved his face closer to the screen. No need, it was coming to him. The black was acquiring a magenta edge, a dark nebulous color. The scientist fumbled inside his desk drawer for a magnifying glass but found only useless office supplies. He took the stapler out and gripped it tightly, releasing a tiny shard of metal to the floor. He pushed it again. It felt right to dispense staples, to waste them.

Plink. Plink, Plink.

Slowly, he could see a mound of pink in the distance, flanked by two bits of white. The mound moved closer, acquired a ridged edge, like whale bones. The darkness lightened, soft shades of purple coming into focus. The scientist remembered his colleague had borrowed the magnifying glass and threw himself towards her desk to fetch it, flinging the stapler across the room. He yanked open a drawer and there it was, the reliable stick and orb. He ran back and bent over his screen, placing the glass over the left edge and then the right, searching. He forgot all about those that might be watching him, those who were in fact watching him with breath held in their throats. What was it he was seeing? Why was he not telling them?

The scientist sat back in his chair.

Huh, he said.

He walked with measured steps back to his colleague's desk. Rummaging through the drawers he found a compact mirror. He sat down in her chair; held the mirror up to his mouth, inspecting his back teeth, the molars. He focused on the uvula, something he never thought much about except that it was an exceptional name for a bodily part. He ran one finger along the back of his mouth, feeling at the ridges, noting their pointy contours. He lowered the mirror, slowly placing it on the desk, and cocked his head to one side. He pushed himself upright, and went back to his computer, brows furrowed as he scratched at his beard. The screen came sharply into focus, the white mounds definitive. As the swinging pink lump propelled itself forward, the scientist collected the bits of information, drew parallels, slotted the new formula together in his mind. He smiled. This was something he had not prepared for, a possibility that never came up. Then he laughed as one unburdened. He laughed until tears streamed from his face, and he put his hands to these tears and wiped but kept at it, hooting as he'd not done in years. The masses, those who were watching, took this as a good sign, and smiled, patted each other on the back. They did not fear the shadow that crept across the room.

The Goddess of Fear

Ivy Grimes

Ivy Grimes is originally from Alabama and now lives in Northern Virginia with her husband and beagle. She is a friendly neurotic person who writes speculative fiction and is looking for more writer friends. She feels nostalgic about her Birmingham writing group that sometimes met at an Applebees where attendees ordered the $1 house beer.

In the Temple of the Goddess of Fear, Thora was safe. She still dreamed of the beast most nights, but the Sisters always heard her screams and came into her room to reassure her. The Sisters told her the beast couldn't enter the Temple. The Goddess of Fear was stronger than the beast. Thora repeated these reassurances to herself each night. *The beast cannot enter. The Goddess of Fear is stronger.*

She'd spent six months with the Sisters, and she tried to repay them for their protection by doing chores for them. The days were clean, with light sparkling through the stained-glass windows. Each morning, she wondered if Jon would return for her, but night always crept up and took away her hope. The days *were* pleasant, though. She was comforted by the gentle rhythms of the work, the slosh of the scrub brush and the swish of linens in the laundry bucket. Since she'd arrived in a panic, running from the beast, she hadn't gone outside. She was afraid that if she stepped past the threshold of the Temple, the beast would smell her and track her there.

It was impossible to think she might lose her refuge. The Sisters wanted her to stay, but the High Priestess of All Goddesses had to approve. The High Priestess hadn't visited the Temple since Thora had arrived, and now she was coming to live with the

Sisters for an entire year. Although Thora stayed in her room when the Sisters performed their most sacred rituals, she knew too much. She was sworn to secrecy, and the Sisters trusted her, but there was reason to believe the High Priestess would not. In all the Temples, religious secrets were closely kept, and outsiders were viewed with suspicion. The Sisters said that the High Priestess guarded her Temples the way snakes guard their nests. As High Priestess, she spent a year at each Temple, rotating through each of the Temples for each of the seven Goddesses. The Temple of the Goddess of Fear was next in her rotation.

Thora hoped to make herself so useful that the High Priestess would see the benefit of keeping her on as a servant. It would have been easier if she agreed to join the order, yet she knew she couldn't officially become one of the Sisters while she still had hope for Jon.

She couldn't think of Jon as the beast or the beast as Jon. Growing up, he'd been the lucky one. Everyone in the village loved him for his wonderful flute-playing at parties and festivals. He made a comfortable income by building small fishing boats. Thora had been the unlucky one, her family dead by the time she was thirteen. One horrible thing after another—accidents and sicknesses and hunger. *No need to relive all that.* She'd been left alone in the house she grew up in, barely sustaining herself by doing other women's laundry. When he'd fallen in love with her, the gossips in the village said she had bewitched him. It was their only explanation for why he'd be drawn to her. She had no doubt that the others in the village blamed her for leaving him, too. Even those who'd known about the beast had thought the problem was Thora's witchery. No one had been willing to take her in for long while the beast was tracking her.

When Jon first started coming around, she'd barely been able to breathe around him. He was so handsome with his flashing eyes and shaggy hair. He'd warned her something was wrong with him, though at the time, he hadn't known just what. She hadn't listened to his warnings.

Forget it. She focused on scrubbing the Temple floors, the smooth blue river pebbles and fragments of sun-bleached bone arranged in dizzying spirals in the thick mortar. Surely the High Priestess would notice how clean everything was and feel the Goddess of the Fear was honored by Thora's simple tasks.

Once the floors were done, her next duty was to rouse Sister Hilde from her afternoon terrors so she could prepare the welcome dinner for the High Priestess. As usual, the rap of her knuckles startled Hilde into shrieking.

After a moment of silence, Hilde answered her in a tremulous voice. "Thank you, Thora. I'll be out in a moment."

After their terrors, the Sisters sounded like dying birds for an hour or so until they recovered. They practiced twice a day. Upon waking and then after lunch, they would work themselves into a state of terror over both mundane and existential threats to the world. By doing so, they were conduits for the Goddess of Fear and could receive her wisdom. Thora knew she wasn't strong enough to bear that kind of wisdom. She'd barely survived the terrors of her own life.

In the kitchen, she peeled the skin from boiled hazelnuts (which the High Priestess was said to be fond of) while Sister Hilde made apple-filled pastries and cut up vegetables to bake with homemade cheese. Hilde was quiet like most of the Sisters, and being in their presence generally made Thora feel like she was resting beside a gentle stream, but on that day, she couldn't stop worrying.

"Is there anything I can do to make the High Priestess more favorable towards me?" Thora asked. "I could give her a list of the chores I do. I could point out that doing these tasks gives the Sisters more time to be afraid."

Sister Hilde grumbled at the description. "We aren't children. We aren't simply afraid. We conjure real horrors and face them—for the sake of the struggling world. Thora, if you joined our Order, it would be much simpler. The High Priestess is wiser than I am, and I can never guess what she's thinking. But I know that joining us would solve these problems."

"I wish I could. This is such a safe place for people who are suffering, and I want to help. I'm happy and useful here. But I can't give up on Jon. He said the wizard could help him. It might take months, but...well." It was no use continuing. The Sisters had no faith in Jon.

"We might not have that much time. The people from your village have come to us in fear of a huge creature they've seen prowling on the edges of the woods at night. So far, he hasn't entered any houses, but who knows how long he'll stay away? When I ask the Goddess, I feel a sense of foreboding."

"He always tries to lock himself inside at night. He tries to protect everyone."

It had been hard to escape from him on those nights when she still thought she could tame him, but she'd been able to climb out of the window each time. As a man, he had been agile enough to dive right through the window and land on his feet, but as a beast, he was too large to fit. He'd broken down the door to come after her. When the morning came, he'd repaired it again.

"He chased you through the woods on three different nights. I've prayed to the Goddess and seen it, Thora. I don't know where you got such energy from, to run until morning." Sister Hilde put down her mixing bowl and took Thora's hand in her floury ones. "There might be some good in him like you say. But there's nothing you can do about it. What will it take for you to let him go?"

But when the morning light arrived, she always found Jon on the forest floor, worn-out and desperate over what he'd done. He had begged her to forgive him. "It wasn't me! It wasn't *really* me."

"Later. I'll think about it later." Thora smiled apologetically at Sister Hilde, who went back to her pastries. The Sisters were so careful with her. Their daily terrors seemed to make them gentler, more compassionate than ordinary people. But the High Priestess took the breath of all seven Goddesses into her nostrils each day, and Thora doubted whether all the other Goddesses were as understanding.

That night when the High Priestess finally arrived and the Sisters lined up in the sanctuary to greet her, Thora tried to hide behind Sister Edith. She peered over Edith's shoulder to stare at the powerful woman whose face and body were mostly obscured by her gray cloak. The High Priestess went down the line putting her hand on each Sister's head in some sort of blessing, and when she got to Sister Edith, she asked Thora to step forward.

"Thora. You are worried about your fate."

Thora closed her eyes and felt the warm hand of the High Priestess on her head.

The High Priestess leaned over and whispered in her ear. "Come see me in the sanctuary after dinner."

She could almost smell the beast's breath again. The scars from the claw-wounds on her shoulders throbbed. She sat as far away from the High Priestess as she could at the table, and she only managed a couple of mouthfuls of food. Night was coming. She knew the beast would smell her if she left the Temple, even if she stayed outside the village. Maybe she could get the High Priestess to give her one more night. Maybe one more night was all Jon needed—just a bit more time to seek out the wizard who cursed him and beg him to reverse the curse.

Instead of helping with the dishes, she slipped out to the sanctuary. The mosaic floors and walls looked holy and solemn in the candlelight. The sight soothed her. The Goddess of Fear was present, wasn't she? She cared for everyone in torment, everyone whose heart was bathed in the acid of oppression. Everyone in danger. As she waited for the High Priestess to arrive, Thora knelt on the rough floor, closed her eyes, and begged the Goddess of Fear to protect her, and to protect Jon, too.

"Why do you care so much about your beast?"

She turned around to find the High Priestess standing behind her. She helped Thora to her feet. She was quieter than Thora had imagined she'd be, her voice barely above a whisper. She didn't sound cruel or kind, and she didn't remove her gray hood so that Thora could see her whole face. All Thora could see were her eyes glittering in the candlelight and that she wasn't smiling.

"I hate the beast, but I love Jon. I made a commitment to him because I loved him. You don't know him. He's—"

The High Priestess laughed, but she didn't sound amused. "I know everyone in this country. The Goddesses show me everything. I know your beast. I know your Jon, too. Jon is a clever man. He's quick like a cat. In fact, he was quicker than your cat."

Thora let out a soundless gasp. It was true, and she'd pushed the memory aside. As the beast, Jon had slaughtered her cat. Her precious Milksop, the golden striped cat she'd loved so long.

"He didn't mean to." It embarrassed her to say this in front of the High Priestess. Didn't she sound like a fool?

"I know he told you it's all the fault of Dominus the wizard. Dominus is no friend of mine, but he didn't curse Jon out of sheer cruelty. Jon went to him and said he wanted to be more than human. He wanted great power. He asked the wizard to touch him with his magic. Dominus isn't known for having great control of his magic, Thora. Jon knew it was a risk, and he took it. Now he is what he is."

The beast wasn't Jon. Of course, the High Priestess knew Thora's thoughts.

"Who is to say who the real Jon is? What is any person? Each of us is our own separate country with deserts and teeming rivers and decaying tree stumps and prismatic leaves."

The High Priestess spoke in riddles. It was the weird way of religion. The Sisters spoke this way too sometimes after their most sacred rituals.

"I don't presume to know the sacred mysteries of life or death," Thora said. "But the Jon I knew was a kind man. I promise he was. Once he even made a splint for a fox with a lame paw. He was so gentle that the fox didn't mind. Maybe that doesn't mean anything to you, but it meant something to me."

"You're brave, Thora. And you're very intelligent. I'm not saying this because I pity you. I never lie."

Thora hadn't thought of herself as brave or intelligent, especially not when she was screaming so hard she thought her lungs would tear as she ran through the woods, listening for the grunt of the beast behind her. Not when she was risking her life night after night, hoping that she and the hidden Jon could somehow tame the beast. Always failing.

The High Priestess pulled Thora into an embrace. She smelled like the sea and simmering tea leaves and smoke. At this proximity, Thora could feel the power of the High Priestess. It was much stronger than the power of the beast.

The High Priestess pulled away again, as remote as she had been before. "I am not a Goddess, Thora. I'm just close to them. I'm a messenger. I've asked the Goddess of Fear if you can remain here—it's her decision, not mine. And she says she wants to meet you first."

"Meet me? I'm here every day." Thora loved the Goddess—she put her love into her chores. But she was afraid. How close did the Goddess want to get to her?

"Closer," the High Priestess whispered.

***

The ceremony was to take place in the sanctuary, but Sister Joan brought a pillow and blanket from Thora's room so Thora would be more comfortable lying on the floor.

It was one of the rituals Thora hadn't been allowed to take part in before. She would drink a concoction prepared by Sister Hilde (who Thora learned was a master of potions as well as pastries), and it would bring on a vision.

She was terrified of the Goddess, but she was also desperate to see her. She had so many questions for her, and she hoped that by gaining wisdom from the Goddess, she might also gain comfort.

Without that, Thora feared she'd spend her whole life waiting for Jon to recover. Now that she was so close to meeting the Goddess, she could admit to herself that she wasn't sure if Jon would ever recover. She didn't really know how much of the beast was Jon or how much of Jon was the beast. But now she would find out.

The potion was both bitter and sweet, like dandelion leaves cut up with strawberries. If she joined the Sisters, maybe she'd learn the secrets of making it. She often helped Hilde in the kitchen.

But Jon. What will happen to him? He'll be alone forever.

As the potion took effect and Thora's eyelids grew heavy, the Sisters gathered around her and sang a song about a turtle-dove and a raincloud. Darkness fell. She felt herself wandering through that darkness, reaching out her hands to try to feel her way, but there was nothing to steady herself against.

A light shone in the distance, and she saw shadows moving in the light. She counted the shadows. Fourteen. Seven Goddesses and seven Gods. They moved. They swayed. Yes, they were dancing. She tried to get closer so she could dance with them, but there was some unbridgeable gap that kept her away. Deep, strange joy crept over her. It was like she wasn't there. No more self. Only happy Goddesses and Gods, united in love before the world was made.

Things changed, though. In the midst of the deities, shadows of two giants appeared. The giants were even taller than the deities. One giant strangled the other and cut up the other's body, and with the parts and pieces, he made the world. The dead giant's head became the earth, his body the sky. The deities circled the world and mourned the dead with a frightful, wheezing song. Yet as they mourned, the new earth teemed with life. The remaining giant shrank himself and walked on the earth spreading the glow of humanity.

The deities had made the giants, hadn't they? They must have known what would happen. The earth was made in violence. Life killed life to sustain itself. The deities celebrated while they mourned and mourned while they celebrated.

One of the shadows approached Thora and walked into a clarifying light. She knew this was the Goddess of Fear. Her body was the color of dried blood, and her eyes and lips sizzled like fire. Her limbs were muscular, and she moved with quick grace.

And her face was divided. When she turned to the left, she was an intent-looking lioness, and when she turned to the right, she was a white-haired and wise old woman. When she sat on the indistinct ground beside Thora, she towered over her. Thora wanted to touch her, but she was afraid. This Goddess lived inside Thora and had tortured her. Yet she had also kept her alive.

When the Goddess shook her head or shifted her body, a breeze blew over Thora carrying the smell of faraway fruit and a thunderstorm. On the horizon, the other deities moved aimlessly, lost without one of their members.

There was so much she wanted to ask, but she didn't know how.

"You want to stay in my Temple," the Goddess said with the music of coins falling over cobblestones. Thora had expected an ominous rumble, but her voice was light and high.

"Yes."

"But for your lover."

"Yes." Something inside her groaned, as if she'd stepped on warped wood. "Is he really so bad?"

The Goddess stared at her as if waiting for her to continue.

Thora unburdened herself. "I have some wonderful memories of him, Goddess. I do love him. But he's been cursed. And I love my life too much to let mine be destroyed before its time."

She hadn't realized that she loved her life until she said it. Yes, she wanted more life, in spite of its difficulties. She didn't want to waste it on the rage of a beast.

"You wonder if Jon is good when each night he transforms into something evil," the Goddess said. "I have seen you in my Temple, and I know you are someone who craves understanding."

Thora nodded, abandoning all modesty.

"Who is good?" the Goddess asked. "The world is bathed in blood. All of our genius and violence went into the creation of the world, and every good thing contains us all, and every bad thing contains us all. Even before mortals, we deities imagined violence and death, and each of us are in each of you. So tell me—how could a simple man be only good? You already know there is evil lurking in the man you love."

Thora listened. The Goddess understood her. She was sitting beside her. She was her friend. For so long, Thora had been afraid to tell herself that Jon was anything but good. Otherwise, she'd have to hold him responsible for the beast.

"If I join the Sisters and end my commitment to Jon, what will happen to him?"

"The same thing will happen to him if you don't leave him. Every night when he changes, he will frighten those he comes in contact with. The fear he inspires will alienate him, and it will likely destroy him."

"Whether I hope for him or let him go?"

"Yes. He has not seen the wizard and begged to be changed back. I do not know if he can be changed back. Either way, he isn't really willing to give up his new power. He feels it protects him from all that's gone wrong."

"What has gone wrong for him? He always seemed so happy before he was the beast."

"I see things you are unable to see. If you join the Sisters in my Temple, then your vision will expand."

Yes! Then she would see the most fearsome visions. She would know daily terror. But at least it would be constructive fear. She could use it to empathize with others, to warn others. Her fears for Jon were for nothing. They were like using a fork and knife to try to eat the wind.

"What do I have to do to join?" Thora asked, and the look on the Goddess's face changed from kind attention to hungry interest.

"You have to fight me," the Goddess of Fear whispered. And her face was no longer divided in two, and she no longer had the body of a woman. She became all lioness, teeth bared and growling. After having befriended Thora and confided in her, now she was treating her like nothing but delicious prey.

"I have no weapon!" Thora cried out, and a knife appeared in her hand.

She and the lioness circled each other, and as Thora's hand trembled, she prayed to all the deities (including the Goddess she fought) to give her strength.

The lioness struck out with a quick paw to Thora's shoulder (a place that had been torn by the beast before), but Thora dodged. She was quicker than she had been. She tried to pretend her knife was a giant claw, and she closed her eyes and slashed at the creature until she made contact. She opened her eyes, and the lioness was gone. The Goddess had returned in her giant, golden form, with her split face. She lay on the ground with her eyes closed, a gash in her side pouring thick, golden blood. Thora ran to her and tried to stop the bleeding, pressing her hands into the gash.

"Did I kill you? Did I kill you?" she shouted. What would the world do without the Goddess of Fear? Thora couldn't live with herself if she was responsible for killing her.

The Goddess's eyes opened, and so did Thora's. She found herself back in the Temple beneath the weight of her blankets. Had it been a dream? When she looked down at her hands, though, she found them still covered with the Goddess's shimmering blood, as if she'd bathed them in liquified gold coins.

The Sisters had crouched down, surrounding her and watching her as she slept. When they saw her stained hands, they celebrated.

"You killed the Goddess!" Sister Hilde cried, embracing Thora. "You're one of us now."

"I'm sorry, I'm so sorry! She told me to fight her." Thora lay her head back down, feeling woozy. The potion was still wearing off. How could her dream have bled into reality and covered her hands?

The High Priestess asked the Sisters to step aside, and she crouched beside Thora's head.

"Each God and Goddess requests something different as part of the initiation. The Goddess of Fear must be fought. She wants you to win. What did she look like for you? For me she was a spider."

Thora tried to explain the split face, and everyone was impressed. With each initiation, the Goddess showed new complexities.

Before Thora rose from her makeshift bed, the Sisters washed her hands in a tub of warm water. The clotted gold softened and pulled away from her skin, the pieces breaking apart and brightening the surface of the water.

"We'll use this to water the flowers," Sister Joan said as she picked the remaining flecks from Thora's hands. "We don't want to waste the essence of the Goddess."

"You can pour out the water and admire the golden flowers that grow. You haven't seen them yet," Sister Hilde said.

Yes, she could go outside now. She'd still be afraid of the beast, but now she'd killed the Goddess. And the Goddess still lived.

She stood up, and though she wanted to cry from some strange mixture of sorrow and joy, she didn't. Jon was gone. She was a Sister. The moon was full when she went outside for the first time in six months to pour the golden water at the roots of the golden flowers. They grew above her head, and each petal was the size of her hand. She grabbed one flower and tugged it to her nose, and the smell was that of the Goddess—thunderstorms and faraway fruit. What a beautiful and horrible Goddess. She let the flower go, and it bobbed on its thick stem. She looked forward to the next day when she would explore the full Temple grounds for the first time.

Thora didn't see the beast outside, and she didn't dream of him that night. The next day dawned with the promise of life. Perhaps the beast did smell her when she went outside, but perhaps the Goddess of Fear held his throat when he crept too close to her temple.

Soul Mate

Paulene Turner

Paulene Turner is an Australian writer of short stories, short plays and novels. A former journalist, she is currently writing a YA series about time travel. She lives in Sydney with her husband, twin daughters and twin pugs. Her work has appeared in publications in Australia, UK and USA. Find more of her stories at pauleneturnerwrites.com

Death was not quite how I imagined it would be.

As a life-long atheist, I'd pictured instant oblivion - a never-ending sleep with no consciousness of anything on earth or in heaven. Not this.

"Breakfast!" My landlady's shouts rocket me awake. "Come and get it! And don't come moanin' and hauntin' me with your grumbling belly if you miss out!"

I climb out of bed, in my private room, in this two-storey mint-green house (strange colour choice, I know), full of old world charm and ghosts. Located in a northern suburb of Sydney, Australia, the house looks like any other on the street. Only the uncut grass (ghosts don't do lawns!), surfeit of spiders' webs, and strange percussive sounds emanating from the upper rooms at night give any clue that the house is haunted. We never stay too long in one place. Last month, we haunted an abandoned house near Reykjavik, Iceland, with views of blue ice and grey whales.

My room is simple - bed, mirror, sink, old-fashioned trunk and use of a shared bathroom (which cleans itself - a heavenly touch.). It's for short stays. More permanent residents have bigger spaces, sumptuous sofas, waterfall taps. How do we all fit into an ordinary suburban house? It seems ghosts take up whatever space they need - in some kind of Tardis-like afterlife magic, as far as I can figure.

All the guests here are In-betweeners - souls suspended somewhere between life and the afterlife. In our backyard are two wooden doors - one dark-toned, one light. We'll all pass through one of these before our journey is done. Which door, and when? That is the question.

But we can't go through either, until those who love us, still among the living, are prepared to let us go.

***

"Mornin' Cassidy!" says the landlady, Maz - short for Marilyn. "A great day to be not-quite-dead, ain't it."

"Sure is."

The sky is blue. There's a hint of jasmine on the breeze. Rainbow lorikeets flit around the branches of a tree outside my window. Not so bad.

I arrived in this realm one night after a long week of work when I fell asleep at the wheel of my car and ploughed, head-on, into a truck.

Cassidy Braithwaite. Loving daughter of Charles and Lena Braithwaite. Treasured fiancé to Vaughan Gallagher. Taken too soon, the headstone said.

Time is fuzzy here, but I'd guess that was around six months ago. Since then, I've become part of this community of souls, in a halfway house between life and death, awaiting eternal placement through one door or ... the other.

"You look a little pale today, Hon." Maz peers at my face. "You feelin' okay?"

"Fine!" I say.

"Well, enjoy the day as if it was your last. Because one day..."

We say it together: "... it will be!"

Maz winks and clicks her tongue, tucking a strand of wavy blonde hair beneath her sailor's cap.

Breakfast is the usual crazy buffet. The rock stars - and there's a lot of them here - start with vodka and orange, followed by rocky road chocolate smothered with marshmallows and Turkish delight. Elvis breakfasts on lobster thermidor and chips the size of doorstops. David Bowie has cappuccino and Italian donuts.

Movie stars generally eat leaner. Humphrey Bogart has ham and eggs, Lauren Bacall, watercress soup. Many of the starlets I recognise from old films stick with black coffee - more from habit than concern about their weight. Everyone in this place stays looking the way they did at their best during the living years.

Shakespeare nibbles an apple as he works on a new play, his quill tucked behind his ear. He calls Maz over to read lines whenever he wants to hear how they flow.

It's a lively, loud community with music, monologues and mania. New people come and go all the time. Few politicians or lawyers spend much time here - some people are easier to let go of than others. But famous actors and musicians, still held close in many living hearts, stick around much longer. Some may never leave.

"Saved you a seat!" Franklin Kent, my halfway house friend, sits at the quieter end of the table. A rock star in the 60s, with twilight blue eyes, and dark hair, shiny as a shampoo ad, Franklin had one song that was a very big hit. After that he slipped into obscurity and eventually died, penniless, in a condemned building in his 50s. He played his hit song for me once ... Meh! Still, someone obviously liked it enough to keep him here all this time.

"So what shall we do today?" Franky asks. "Feel like spooking a few churches, give the old pastors a thrill? Or shall we visit our enemies, whisper sour nothings in their ears and make them spill their cappuccinos."

He grins and a dimple appears in his right cheek, giving me a hint of why teenage girls and guys used to weep and faint at his concerts.

"Any of your enemies still above ground must surely be in nursing homes," I say, "and we ought to leave the poor blighters alone. Anyway, shouldn't we be thinking of good deeds to raise our profile with"--I point upwards--"and move us closer to the right door."

"Ah, but which door is the right one?" Franky whispers. "Not sure any of these rock stars will think an eternity of harp music such a great prospect."

"You two behave now, won't you?" Maz winks as we depart. "Never know who's watching!"

"Marilyn dear! I nee-eed you!" Shakespeare trills.

"Coming, Will!" Maz shrugs. "For my sins!" She heads over to confer with the Bard.

As I raise my hand in farewell, Franky grabs my arm and holds it up to the light, his expression grim. He doesn't need to say it. My arm, my whole body, is more transparent today than it was yesterday. We both know what that means.

My fiancé, Vaughan, is preparing to move on.

***

"I really thought he loved me," I shout to Franky as we float above the highrise buildings and stunning harbour of Sydney.

"He did. He does," Franky insists. "This doesn't mean he's forgotten you. You're still in his heart."

"It's that woman he met at the client party. I knew it! Cheating bastard."

"Shhhh!" Franky points upwards in warning.

"I don't care who hears!" I shout as I dive head-first between the office buildings and begin swooping in and out of the city traffic. The cool wind feels good on my face. A car's brakes screech behind me - one of the more ghost-aware drivers has detected my presence. I look back and see Franky shaking his head in disapproval.

"I would never have let him go so quickly," I yell over the traffic noise.

"And that would be good, how?" Franky demands, catching up. "Do you want to stay in the halfway house forever?"

Franky grips my hand, and leads me through the maze of city streets to a park overlooking Sydney harbour and the Opera House, where he deposits me on the grass.

"It's all right for you," I say. "You sing one song in your twenties, and people love you eternally. You get heaps of time to build up your goodwill points."

"Maybe," Franky leans back, head on his hands. "But I was

a rock star. Lots of drugs, and meaningless sex. I have a lot of catching up to do."

I huff and lop off the head of a purple agapanthus flower nearby. Because I can. Franky taught me how to 'contact' earthly things. And I'm getting quite good at it. Though, strictly speaking, we're not supposed to touch anything outside the house.

"And the fans don't 'love' me the way Vaughan loves you," he says. "They don't know me. If they did know the real me ... well, I would have shot through the doorway to the dark place decades ago."

Unable to stay still, I levitate and drift about, eavesdropping on earthly conversations. A mum playing I Spy with her kid. A man getting heated on a business call. I catch a snippet of romance by the pond.

"I adore you," a chunky man in his twenties tells a woman, stroking her dark hair. They drift forward to kiss, but I zoom between them, screeching: "He says that now! But as soon as another hot girl or guy comes along, he'll forget all about you!"

The lovers rear back in confusion. "Your lips are ice cold," the woman says, touching her mouth.

"Oh, for Heaven's sake!!" Franky seizes my arm and hauls me into the clouds, so fast I think I might throw up. Given I don't have any stomach contents, that would be quite an achievement.

"Don't throw away points like that, Cassidy! You're acting like a spoilt child!"

I pout and try to pull away, but he keeps hold of me as we float back to the ground, to an empty bus-stop I know well - because it was the one nearest the apartment where I lived with Vaughan.

"Why don't we go see your fiancé," Franky says. "Find out what's happening."

"Good idea."

"But you have to stay calm. Promise?"

"Promise."

***

Moonlight spills through partly open blinds revealing a modern apartment with a plethora of framed pictures of Vaughan and me. One picture, I note, is slightly askew. I use my 'contact' skills to fix it.

"What are you doing?" Franky whispers.

"Just tidying up. Why are we whispering?"

A male voice echoes along the hallway. Like seaweed on a stream, we drift through the air, into Vaughan's bedroom. He's on his usual side of the bed, in a circle of lamplight as he talks on the phone.

"All right, just a couple of drinks then... Marble Bar, six o'clock? Okay. I'm looking forward to it, too."

As he hangs up, he has this self-satisfied look on his face. I catch a glimpse of a woman's picture on the phone screen. Too smiley. Too pretty. Too alive.

"CHEATER!" I hurl at him.

Vaughan gasps and looks around, holding his breath as his eyeballs swivel in their sockets.

"Did he hear me?" I whisper.

Franky signals that I should follow him out and back to the living room.

"He can sense you," he says. "When you've had a strong connection during life, there is sometimes a lingering intra-dimensional awareness."

"Did you see his face when he was talking to her?" I study my arm in the darkness. "I feel more like the invisible woman every second."

"Don't you want him to move on, Cassidy? Have a life, some happiness, while he's still among the living?"

"Yes, of course, but..." I sigh as I try to order my thoughts. "I just thought it would last longer ... the love we had. I still feel it. Why doesn't he?"

Franky presses his lips together but stays quiet.

"I guess I'm not ready ... to let him go," I admit.

Franky nods, sadly, before exiting through the brick wall - which still freaks me out. I do the same and we drift through the air, like two clouds, surfing the breeze.

"Hmmm. They're meeting at the Marble Bar," I say. "I know where that is."

Franky's dark brows form a tight single line. "Not a good idea, Cassie."

"Neither was driving home when I was so tired after that monster week at work. But I did it anyway. Because I wanted to see Him. Vaughan. The love of my life."

I died for him. I figure he owes me a smidge more than six months of grieving.

**

The next night, Franky accompanies me to witness Vaughan's first date since my death. Despite my strong suggestions that 'I'll be fine on my own!' and attempts to give him the slip on the way there, Franky's Hell-bent on keeping watch over me.

It's Friday evening and the Marble Bar is buzzing with city workers celebrating the end of the business week. Men in suits and women in skirts and high heels slurp down alcohol in the dazzling rococo room - all marble and gold, with leadlights in the ceiling. I double take when I get my first glimpse in a mirror behind the bar and see everything in the room perfectly reflected back, except Franky and me.

"Yeah, a bit weird, that," Franky says, noting my expression. "Not sure I'll ever get used to it."

Vaughan's already perched on a barstool. It was always his habit to arrive early; he never wanted anyone to be uncomfortable, wondering if he'd show.

He's nervous, slurping his beer and trying to read the news on his phone as his gaze ricochets back to the entry. Looking for Her.

A cluster of backs block his view as she comes in. And, suddenly, she's right there, in front of him. He gives her a way too big smile - revealing, at least to me, that he's nervous. His uneasiness doesn't recede when she sits down.

"Well, this is ... awkward," Franky says, watching the pair make stilted small talk. Vaughan's hands can't settle; he's probably craving a cigarette to make himself appear more at ease, though he gave up smoking years ago.

"I can't watch this," Franky says. "I think I'll give them some space. Over there. Wanna join?"

"No, I'm good."

Floating through the crowd - and I do mean through the crowd - Franky leans on the bar next to a stunning redhead sitting alone. She's not young - late 30s or even early 40s is my guess - but she definitely has something. Guts to come on her own, for one. And a style born of confidence. Is that Franky's type?

He moves behind her and gently blows on her neck. The few strands of hair that have escaped her stylish chignon dance about. Patting them down, the woman glances around suspiciously.

Franky leans on his elbow making gooey eyes at her. "Where have you been all my life? And Death," he says.

"Wow that line is so old ... almost as old as you," I call out.

Franky scratches his cheek, middle finger up, for my benefit.

"Okay, then," he begins again. "How about ...What's a nice girl like you doing in a ...?" He stops, looks around, frowns. "What am I saying? This is a nice place, you definitely fit in here."

"But who let you in?" I shout. From this angle, Franky's eyes are full of reflected light; they seem so alive, it's hard to believe he's not.

"I'm glad you came out tonight." Words from Vaughan's date - Brittany - call me back to the reason I'm here.

"I'm glad I came, too." Vaughan replies. Lame, lame. I almost want to coach him to a better response.

"I didn't think you would." Brittany sips her Kir Royale, a sparkling red concoction in a champagne glass.

"Well, it's just a couple of drinks."

From the tight smile Brittany gives, I see she's disappointed; she was hoping for more. I smell her perfume - too much - and note her perfect nails, and make-up. I'm betting she's wearing shapewear to hold her stomach flat, too. She's gone all out tonight. Like a fisherman who preps his boat and supplies carefully before going after a big catch. She's a predator, I decide. Not right for him.

Vaughan keeps looking around, brow creased, as if he senses me here.

"Are you expecting someone?" Brittany asks.

"No."

"Step back," Franky shouts. "Give him some room."

I take a small step away and give my friend my innocent-not innocent smile in response. He shakes his head slowly in warning.

After the first glass, things loosen up between Vaughan and Brittany. They manage to have an animated conversation about holidays. When she says she'd like to go to Croatia, he freezes.

"Have you been there?" she asks.

"Yeah," he says. With me. "It's lovely." We had one of our best holidays there. Brittany waits for him to say more, but the conversation stops cold.

Meanwhile, Franky is reading the phone screen over the

redhead's shoulder, his hand resting on her arm. Almost as if she detects something, she puts her hand over his. The two of them look quite cosy together.

"Back off Romeo!" I call out.

He winks and continues to read. Which I find unaccountably irritating.

My ghostly hackles rise further as Brittany raises the subject of Vaughan "losing someone close." He stares fixedly into his glass, a muscle twitching along his jawline as he clenches his teeth.

Finally, he says: "I'd rather not talk about it, if that's okay?"

"Sure, no worries."

I almost feel sorry for Her. Until I realise that I've now been dispensed with as a topic. Forgotten. The mood eases between them, their unspoken agreement that there'll be no more talk of the dead; it's time to focus on the living.

"What do you say, we leave them to it?" Franky is back at my shoulder.

"Not yet."

I watch Brittany laughing and wonder how many sets of braces it took to get her teeth looking that perfect.

"You thirsty?" I ask Franky. "Because I am."

Brittany has a fresh glass and I really fancy a taste. (For some reason, we only have beer and whisky at the Halfway House.) I position my face over her glass and look up at Franky, who watches darkly. Then I use all my ghostly focus and contact powers to slurp up a huge sip. I drain a third of the glass in one sip, too fast - some of it goes up my nose. I giggle and wipe it away.

"That's funny," Brittany says, looking at her drink. "I could have sworn I had a full glass."

That makes me laugh even harder. Franky doesn't seem amused. Not then. Nor when I wave my arm, the way he taught me, and knock her drink all over her.

"What the-?" Brittany looks around for someone to blame, but no one's there. "I'm not sure how that happened ..." she wipes drink from her clothes. "I'll just ... I'll be back." She heads to the bathroom.

"What did that achieve?" Franky folds his arms, annoyed.

"It made me feel good."

"What about Vaughan? Does he feel good?"

My fiancé appears less than relaxed as he takes up his phone and looks at a picture of the two of us together.

"Yes!" I fist-pump the air. "He still wants me!"

He looks at a few more pics, then puts the phone down and glances towards the bathroom.

"Don't stop! There's more!" I shout at him. "What about the Croatian pics? Why don't you check them out?"

I hold my arm up to the light. It's fainter than before.

"I guess the date's going better than I thought," I say. "What do I do?"

"I could boost up his memories of you," Franky says. "That will give you a little more time to get your head around this."

"Really?" I nod.

Franky stands in front of Vaughan, closes his eyes, takes a breath and gently exhales. Eventually, he's expelling grey smoke, which envelops Vaughan completely. When the mist clears, Vaughan rubs his eyes and picks up the phone, scrolling in earnest through pictures of the two of us.

But they don't make him happy. He seems more disturbed than ever. Breathing heavily, he glances toward the powder room and leaves.

I'm shocked. He'd never leave anyone hanging like that! I'm not sure how I feel about it.

When Brittany returns, she finds his empty seat and a fifty dollar bill on the bar for drinks.

"Fuck!" she says, which makes me smile.

"Our work here is done."

***

The next morning, I'm whole again. As solid as the rock stars howling into their mugs and drumming on the breakfast setting.

"Morning honey," says Maz. "Another beautiful day ... to be halfway."

"Sure is!"

Hungrier than usual, I order eggs and toast. It's delicious. Even the usual morning racket today seems amusing when I'm usually tearing my hair out by now.

Franky seems quiet. "Good to have you back," he whispers.

"Good to be back," I say. "She wasn't right for him."

"Probably not," Franky agrees. "But I guess we'll never know now, will we?"

I ask him what he did last night to boost up Vaughan's memories of me. At first he doesn't want to tell me, but I keep at him. I'm no quitter.

"I just shared some images of you with him," he says. "The way your hair looks with a backdrop of stars. How your eyes swirl like the Milky Way when you're happy. How your laughter sounds like the cascade of coins into a poker machine tray when you've had a big win."

"Oh, right."

I'm a ghost, but I still feel kind of funny at the moment.

"You know," he adds, "soppy stuff to stimulate the romantic memories."

Soppy stuff? I nod.

"Franky, Cassie, want a part in a play?" Maz calls out. Shakespeare is coaching Maz in a monologue from his new work (with a woman in the lead).

"We don't want to show you up," Franky says.

"In your dreams," Maz winks.

"Marilyn, focus," says Shakespeare. "Now in this scene, the

woman is fighting the whole patriarchy. But does she back down? No. She's prepared to die for the principles she believes in."

Wow! I have goosebumps... which, for a ghost, is really something!

"You know in the time when I was popular ..." Franky begins.

"For five minutes ..." I clarify.

"Well, in those five minutes, a famous director asked me to play Romeo in a film."

"You? Romeo?"

"Yeah. But I was such an arrogant pratt, I didn't even show up for the audition."

Franky as Romeo? He certainly had the look, or so his fans would say.

"Shall we look in on Vaughan, this evening?" he asks.

"Yeah."

***

As night descends, we return to the flat. Vaughan's sitting up at the breakfast bar, scrolling through pictures of us. He must have started straight after work because he's still in his suit, though he's thrown his tie on the floor. I always hated him doing that.

He looks perturbed as he scrolls, but stops and smiles at an image of us swimming in the clear Adriatic sea. I bet he's remembering the funny little man who insisted on taking our photo that day. The guy was so old and quirky, it was hard to believe he'd ever seen a mobile phone, much less knew how to use one. But he took heaps of shots and they turned out to be some of the best of the holiday. Vaughan and I both chuckle at the same time.

"I'll wait outside," says Franky, "give you two some privacy."

My fiancé tenses and looks around the room, as if he's heard something.

"Why did you leave me?" he whispers.

"I didn't want to," I said. "I still don't."

He gulps down the rest of his wine and refills the glass with the little that's left in the bottle. "Why?" he says more loudly. Demanding an answer.

For a moment the barrier between our worlds feels gossamer thin. He fixes his intense gaze on me, as if he sees me there.

"There's no answer! There's no reason. It just happened," I say.

"There has to be an answer!" he shouts.

The ting of an incoming phone message breaks the spell. He snaps the phone up. It's from Brittany.

-Just checking you're okay?

-Sorry about last night, he types.

-Was it something I said?

 -No. I had an emergency.

-What emergency?

He flings the phone onto the sofa and gulps down more wine. Then starts to open another bottle.

"Haven't you had enough?" I say.

He turns to me. "Don't you start! I'm just getting started!"

There's no talking to him when he's like this. His sweet, easy-going nature turns sour and incendiary.

I can't watch this.

I head back through the wall and find Franky waiting at the edge of the bay. The water is still tonight. And really dark. Is it that dark behind the second door?

"Thought you'd be a while longer" he said.

"I'll go back when he's run out of wine."

Franky raises his eyebrow and nods.

"She texted him," I say.

"Really? Few choice words, I imagine, for standing her up?"

"No, she seemed quite calm." Calmer than I would have been.

"We might need to boost up his memories of you again," says Franky. "But it works best if he's asleep, so ... shall we come back later?"

"Okay."

Will we have to do this every night? I wonder. To stop me winking out like a burnt-out star.

"And in the meantime...!" Franky grins mischievously and shoots off, a silver streak against the liquorice sky. I follow.

He heads towards the city at speed, making his way to the busy bars around Circular Quay.

"What are we--"

Diving down to ground level, he zooms right through a group of drunken men in suits, before flying up again, clutching a wallet.

"You picked someone's pocket?"

Franky grabs a wad of cash, then drops the wallet. The guys below snatch it up. "Steve, found your wallet!"

"What do you want money for? We can't spend it!" I say.

"We can't, but ..."

Franky's off again. I follow him to a city park where a homeless woman is bunking down on a bench, surrounded by plastic bags.

"Hey!" he calls, letting a couple of large notes flutter down like snowflakes, to land at her feet. She picks up the money, looks up and smiles.

"Can she see us?"

He just keeps flying. I try to keep up.

It's a wild night. We make more 'magic' money-drops at several places. When he sees a man sitting alone on a bench, he swoops down and sits beside him. Just sits, sharing the silence. It's weird, but somehow I can sense the guy's sadness ebbing. "Is that you, Evelyn?" The man strains to see through the air.

We fly over the city, observing life beneath us. A small girl points upwards. "Look mummy, those people are flying."

"Kids and dogs can sense things others don't," Franky says. "Want an ice cream?"

At a late-night stall, a buyer reaches for a pink cone, but Franky whips it out of his grasp. The man and the seller look up. "Wow! Did you see that! The wind just took it!"

"Must be some strong updraft!"

Franky lets some cash drop. The seller catches it. "The wind taketh and it giveth too!"

I can't stop laughing. This is the most fun I've had since ... ever.

"Isn't haunting meant to be scary?" I splutter.

"Depends on the ghost."

We fly down to a party on a boat on Sydney Harbour, and bop away to some wild music. As Franky sings along with a song, I wince. "And you used to be a pop star?" I shake my head. "I guess it was the sixties!"

"Come here you!"

He chases me around the deck. I laugh and whoop and somehow manage to knock a pink cocktail off a tray. The waiter looks around, spooked, as he tries to figure out how that happened.

"Oops!" I say.

"Wanna have some real fun?" Franky asks, darting off before I answer. We head out to the Sydney casino, making straight for a busy roulette table.

Franky goes round the table studying each player. "Who do you like?"

"What do you mean? Who do I think will win?"

"No, who do you like?"

I pick a middle-aged guy, down on his luck. He places his last chip on the number 7.

"Watch this," says Franky. The silver ball rolls around and stops, and Franky quickly snatches it up and moves it to number 7.

"Yes!" The man goes wild as chips pile up in front of him. "Let it ride! I'm feeling lucky tonight!"

We both shake our heads but don't wait to see what happens.

"Not sure you did that guy a favour," I say as we fly back over the harbour.

"Vaughan's probably sleeping now," Franky says. "We can do the smoke if you like."

Vaughan? I'd almost forgotten about him.

"Let's go."

***

We fly across the Sydney Harbour Bridge. From up above, the rows of cars resemble a Motherboard, with colourful pieces fitted together on a metal grid. Then we head west.

Passing through the warm brick walls of Vaughan's flat, we find my fiancé face-down on the floor, whimpering. His glass of red wine has spilt and soaked into the pale carpet. Images of us are playing on a slideshow on his TV screen.

Franky and I sit on the sofa and watch the moments of our lives scroll by. Of Vaughan and me on holidays. At my birthday party with friends. Celebrating after he'd won a big case. On a weekend in the Hunter Valley vineyards where we first said the 'L' word to each other.

"You had fun together," says Franky. "I never had anyone ... special ... like that. I was too cool for just one person. Had to spread the love." The words don't go with his tone of self-loathing.

"Yeah, we were lucky," I say.

"But at least I never had to say goodbye to anyone I loved."

I squat down and look at Vaughan, red in the face, teeth wine-stained, murmuring 'Why?' over and over.

Concentrating, I manage to gently stroke his hair. It seems to comfort him. "There's no reason. Just bad luck."

"Something tells me he won't need any more reminders of you tonight," Franky says.

Near Vaughan's hand on the floor is his mobile phone, and the last text he typed. Still waiting to go.

Franky squats down to read it. "It's to Brittany."

-Sorry, can't meet you. Too soon. Please don't call again.

My ghost friend's expression is serious. "Shall I press Send?"

Yes. "No."

Seeing Vaughan like this makes me feel so ashamed. Of myself. For choosing this for him. For someone I loved. Love. Will always love. But no matter how much I still feel it, and want it to continue, it can't.

Franky's distracted by the pictures on the screen. He smiles at a couple of me and Vaughan with his sister's French bulldog. Then turns his watery eyes to me, more earnest than I've seen him: "I'm so sorry for your loss."

"Me too."

We had fun tonight, Franky and I. It doesn't mean I love Vaughan any less. It's just adjusting to a new reality. Moving on. He needs to move on. And so do I.

"Is there any way to undo the smoke thing you did?" I ask. "Reverse it. Make him forget me more quickly?"

"I can dim his memories of you." Franky grasps my hand. "But I could never make him forget you, Cassie. No matter what else happens, who he's with, part of you will always be with him. Here." He touches his chest. "Just as he'll always be with you."

I kneel down over the phone and focus my ghostly powers on the keyboard - deleting his message to Brittany and composing a different one.

-Let's try again. Promise I won't run away.

Franky is unusually still as he watches me. "Are you sure?"

I nod. Then lean down and whisper in Vaughan's ear: "Goodbye, my love." I manage to graze his cheek with my ghost lips.

Then I hit Send.

***

I'm almost invisible now. More a suggestion of a spook than an actual spectre. I watch Will Shakespeare rehearse the new play with Maz. The two of them get pretty fired up and shout a lot over artistic differences, but it's worth it for Maz's performance, which is transcendent. I always knew she had it in her.

Meanwhile, Frank Sinatra is giving my Franky singing lessons —which, in my opinion, he needs. Though, as I watch him sing the Sinatra song I've Got You Under My Skin, I feel ghostly tears cooling my cheeks.

"Can we fly around a bit more?" I ask. One last time.

He takes me to the top of the Sydney Harbour Bridge where we sit on the highest platform and take in the sweep of the sparkling harbour. I inhale the cool air, a potpourri of sea and car fumes in the deep twilight of the evening. Around us, city lights wink on like fairy fires in the tall buildings. We look down at a super long staircase, where a new group of bridge climbers is just getting started.

"And we didn't have to walk up all those steps to get here," he says.

"Thank God!" I say with feeling, then slap my hand over my mouth, looking heavenwards. And we giggle like naughty children.

"Did you enjoy the halfway house?" Franky asks.

"Yea-ah. But, you can have too much of a good thing."

"The morning jazz jams?" he asks.

"The swearing."

"Afternoon rock jams?"

"The swearing."

"The all-night no-idea-what-I'm-playing jams?"

"And how bad will it be when Mick Jagger and Keith Richards show up?" I ask.

Franky mimes lifting himself up by an invisible noose, tongue out. It makes me smile. He's learnt a few ghostly tricks in his long stay in between worlds.

"You know, now that I really look at you, I think I remember my Mum had a crush on you when she was young."

He shrugs. "What's not to love?"

And then there's this silence, filled up by a ghostly howl as the wind swirls around us and random voices drift up from the street.

"How long will it be, do you think, before your fans let you go through the door?" I ask.

"My fan," he corrects me. "Singular. There's only one left. Betty. She's 74, lives alone. Has a shrine to my memory. Though it's really her own memory of happier times she can't let go of."

"So why don't you work the forgetting smoke on her. Then you can move on" - I pause, before adding - "with me."

I'll feel a lot braver going through the door, if he's beside me.

And now I discover that, yes, ghosts can blush.

Franky takes my hand and ghost-kisses it. He's pretty good at it, so it feels like a normal kiss. "I'd go through any doorway, with you. Dark, light. Whichever one you pass through, is the one for me."

"So come with me, then."

He shakes his head sadly: "I can't take that memory away from Betty. Life's been no picnic for her. I'm all she has."

*　*　*

By the time we get back to the house, I'm barely an outline.

And Maz is waiting for me. "It's time," she says.

As I head into the garden, I look up at the faces of rock stars, and famous movie stars at the windows, gazing down at me with fear and longing in their eyes. Some of them may never get to this point.

Waiting before the two doors, I take a last glance back at Franky's window. He waves and winks from above, then opens his window and blows me a kiss. Which I feel.

I touch my cheek. "See you soon," I whisper.

He might look like the same vain selfish pop star he was back in his time. But he's long past that.

"Whatever door opens, that's the one you have to go through," Maz says.

My mouth is suddenly dry. This is it.

"Don't worry if the pale door doesn't open. It's not the end of the world," she whispers.

"Really?"

And Marilyn Monroe gives me the incandescent smile which made her so famous, and winks. "Some like it hot."

The Best Pierogi in Kocierba

Agnieszka Halas

Agnieszka lives in Lublin, Poland. A former expat who once aimed for a career in biological sciences, then changed her mind, she now works as a translator and writes when she can. As of March 2022, her published works in Polish comprise six novels, two story collections and over thirty short stories. She's also one of the foreign fiction editors at "Nowa Fantastyka", the only Polish speculative magazine that still survives in paper form.

Whether you arrive in Kocierba by bus, car or train, the Glass Mountain immediately catches the eye. It glitters above the meadows and wooded hills, amazingly, surreally beautiful. A marvel of nature, unique on the global scale, a UNESCO World Heritage Site since 1978.

Geologists will tell you it was created by a local volcanic anomaly during the Alpine orogeny. They'll point out the similarities between our Glass Mountain and the famous Obsidian Cliff in Yellowstone National Park or the less-known obsidian mountain near Tulelake in California, although the Glass Mountain's clear greenish glass has a different chemical composition. However, some people believe it was created by extraterrestrial beings, by one of the Catholic saints, or by God himself.

There's also that old fairy tale we all read as children. Its best-known version tells about a king who sought a brave husband for his lovely daughter. He ordered a huge mountain to be erected out of glass. A golden castle was built on the summit for the princess to live in, and the king promised her hand in marriage to whoever would manage to climb there first.

Many young men tried to scale the mountain and failed. Their bones littered the ground below. Finally, after seven years, the princess died of grief. Soon afterwards, her father's lands were invaded and razed by the ruler of a neighboring kingdom, whose son had perished on the Glass Mountain.

A trace content of copper and boron ions gives its steep slopes an aquamarine tint. They're smooth, gleaming, and wickedly slippery. At the beginning of the 20th century, when mountaineering came into fashion in Poland, several climbers met their death here. Today, any attempt at climbing off the marked trail will result in a sky-high fine. Tourists can easily reach the Glass Mountain's summit via a flight of primitive yet sturdy wooden stairs. You'll find similar ones in the Slovakian Tatras, in the upper section of the trail to the Sedielko pass. In Kocierba, though, the stairs start at the bottom of the mountain and lead right up to the top. The climb takes around one and a half hours: a boring but perfectly safe trudge.

If the golden castle ever existed, it's gone now. At the top of the Glass Mountain, there's an observation deck for tourists, complete with a souvenir booth and a coin-operated telescope. Two portable toilets stand off to one side. They spoil the magic of this place somewhat, but hey, life has its necessities.

Some versions of the legend say the castle on the Glass Mountain was surrounded by a garden, in the midst of which grew a magical apple tree. Its fruit healed wounds and guaranteed eternal youth. If you think this sounds familiar, you're right. A wonderful tree with golden apples appears in myths from different parts of the world. In reality, the Glass Mountain has always lacked vegetation. The glass is smooth, untouched by erosion, without so much as a centimeter of soil. Only a historic Art Nouveau sculpture stands just above the observation deck: an apple tree with stylized, wavy branches and a falcon perched on one of them. It's not as showy, though, as the fire-breathing Wawel Dragon statue in Cracow.

I'm resting on the observation deck, the late morning sun warming my back. In clear weather the view from this place is absolutely fantastic; makes you want to spread your wings and fly.

My phone rings. I answer eagerly, hoping for some good news. No such luck.

"Hello, Paweł, unfortunately Alior Bank has rejected our request for remission of interest and penalties. We're still waiting for Crédit Agricole to communicate their decision, but I wouldn't expect a miracle."

I curse softly. Obviously, the debt settlement company isn't to blame; they're doing their best to help us. It's not their fault the case is complicated, involving huge sums of money, and the creditors are reluctant to make concessions. Trying hard to stay calm, I thank the company representative, and then we arrange an appointment next week "to discuss our further strategy".

After ending the conversation, I stare at my phone, wondering how to tell mom that we're back to square one yet again.

***

My father used to work at the big bus factory in Sanok. Day after day, decked out in a respiratory mask and a protective coat, he'd spray varnish onto metal bus bodies. My mother always called him a "man with no ambition." He died of leukemia just before I graduated from high school. Two years later, when I was studying history at the Jagiellonian University (I'd unsuccessfully applied for a major in psychology), my mother remarried. Her second husband was intelligent and enterprising: a man of success. Or so she thought.

My stepfather ran a construction company. Business went quite well until a dishonest contractor cheated him out of a large sum. My stepfather foolishly tried to manage outstanding investment loans by opening more lines of credit, and his company ultimately went bankrupt. The total amount of money owed to the Social Insurance Institution, the Tax Office and five different banks was horrendous.

All the company's assets were auctioned off. My stepfather's large condo, heavily mortgaged, had to be sold. He emigrated to Norway to find work and pay off at least some of his debts, and died a year later of a heart attack. My mother, though, is still paying for his mistakes and her ignorance, since she'd co-signed some of his loans. She now works for an insurance firm, and a debt collector takes a large chunk of her income every month. The remainder is barely enough to live on.

Luckily, we've managed to hold on to our old family home in the small town of Sanok; my mother had signed it over to me just before disaster hit. She lives there now, and I rent a one-room apartment in Cracow. With the debt settlement company's help, I'm trying to negotiate with the remaining creditors in my mother's name, since her request for consumer bankruptcy was rejected in court.

The phone rings again. This time, the name on the display feels like a hammer hitting my head.

"Hi, Inga," I say calmly, even though I'm shaking inside. I don't want to talk with her, or hear what she has to say. The last email she sent was more than clear enough. And I understand where she's coming from, I really do. I know my mother is head over heels in debt, while I'm pushing 30 with a nearly empty savings account, living in a rented apartment the size of a matchbox and driving a clunker bought extra cheaply from a friend. And yes,

I'd been adamant about not quitting my job in Cracow to move with her to Gdansk, where Inga will be starting doctoral studies in October; there's no guarantee I'd find work there, and I have to keep helping my mother. "You didn't care enough about this relationship" was Inga's tough verdict.

My ex mentions her clothes and other possessions still lying around in my apartment. I politely tell her I'm in Kocierba now, so she can retrieve her stuff after the weekend. My calmness seems to irritate her, almost as if she expected me to sound desperate, or even beg her to change her mind. But at the end of the day she's moving to Gdansk, I'm going to stay in Cracow, and she always said a long-distance relationship is out of the question "because trust would be too much of an issue." The conclusion is self-evident, and seriously, I wouldn't have blamed Inga for the breakup, she just didn't have to pour out her grievances as a parting shot.

I disconnect the call, slip the phone back into my pocket, and look around. Even though the Glass Mountain is usually a favorite destination for school trips and parents with noisy children, today the observation deck is empty. The sun is July-hot rather than May-warm, the glass crags already radiating heat. I sit down in the shade of the Art Nouveau apple tree, its apples as big as bread loaves, and muse about how I'd love to just get away from everything. Fly off into the azure like the birds now flitting back and forth in the cloudless sky. I feel like the bronze falcon above my head: heavy, powerless, permanently chained to one bough.

***

The wooden souvenir booth does its best to tempt tourists with dozens of gaudy trinkets: key chains, fridge magnets, plates, ashtrays and mugs, all decorated with images of the Glass Mountain.

Mineral water, soft drinks, chewing gum and chocolate bars complete the assortment.

"Hi, how can I help you?"

The vendor is my mother's age, perhaps slightly younger. Gaunt and weathered, she looks like a lifelong nicotine addict. Her hair is short and dyed blonde, probably to hide grey streaks. Her tired smile only deepens the lines at the corners of her eyes and mouth.

"I'd like a small bottle of mineral water, uncarbonated, and two Mars bars, please."

Chocolate bars are more expensive up here than in Kocierba. Oh well, I should have remembered to bring something to eat. I didn't intend to stay this long on the Glass Mountain, I only came up here to sit on the observation deck for a bit. Weirdly, though, now that I've scaled all those steps, I don't feel like leaving, perhaps because there are no tourists in sight and the view is truly breathtaking, the sky over our heads a pure, unblemished blue, with only a cloud or two on the horizon. Crisscrossing white lines mark the trails of planes bound for destinations I'll probably never visit.

"Do you know why it's so empty here today?"

"No idea." The woman looks around in surprise, as if taking note of the fact for the first time. "Maybe there's something going on in town? A festival?"

"You don't live in Kocierba?"

"No, in Rzepedz." She eyes me with curiosity. "And where are you from?"

"Cracow." I slip the change into my wallet, then unwrap one of the chocolate bars and take a large, sticky-sweet bite.

"Is this your first visit here?" asks the vendor, obviously bored and eager to chat.

Out of politeness I force myself to exchange a few more words with her. I learn that her husband died several years ago, and that her son got a computer science degree and emigrated to Sweden. My phone rings again, so I apologize and step aside. It's my mom, sobbing.

"Paweł, I'm at my wits' end, the debt settlement people have phoned..."

I sigh. Struggling to keep my patience, I say some comforting platitudes. My mother is undergoing treatment for depression (no wonder), but she just seems to sink deeper into despair and resignation with every passing year. She could probably get a second job, but I don't have the nerve to suggest it. She's nearly at retirement age and it's easy to understand why she's not bending over backward to pay down debts she didn't incur.

***

It's 2:00 P.M., the sun still bright and hot, the observation deck still empty. I'm sitting in the shade of the bronze apple tree, wondering why on earth I'm the only tourist on the Glass Mountain today. Not that I'm complaining. The souvenir vendor is probably less happy.

I remember coming here with my parents when I was little. My mother would spread sunscreen on her shoulders and cleavage, then anoint me as well. I hated that. We'd sit down on the deck, and my father would take out his binoculars.

"Look, a hawk," he'd say, pointing at the birds circling over the forest. Or: "Look over there, the ravens have smelled carrion." I'd nod distractedly, staring at the clouds.

As a boy, I used to fantasize that I'd become a pilot. Or a mountain climber. Or, best of all, a traveler. An explorer of distant lands, winning fame and glory. Stupid, futile dreams of an eight-year-old, unaware of his limitations, blissfully ignorant of the fact that all the tantalizing secrets of our planet have already been laid bare. The world has shrunk. Neither a trip to the summit of Mount Everest nor an expedition to the North Pole will impress anyone these days.

Years later, in the hospital, my father told me: "Paweł, life is the art of giving up on dreams." His words made me angry at the time, but now I know what he meant.

***

It's nearly 6:00 P.M. The sun is low in the sky, the air getting cooler. The shadows are lengthening, and I'm still sitting on top of the Glass Mountain. I've drunk the bottled water and eaten both chocolate bars, I have nothing with me except my wallet, an umbrella and a lightweight jacket. Even so, I make no move to leave.

I've turned my phone off because I don't want any more calls today, either from Inga or from my mother. I'm too tired to drive back to Cracow, but I don't have the energy to search for a hotel in Kocierba. I think I'll spend the night here, under the statue of the magical apple tree that only existed in legends. Who knows, perhaps I'll wake up in another world, in the garden by the golden castle?

The click of a key being turned interrupts my thoughts. The souvenir vendor has just locked her booth. She glances in my direction, then approaches.

"Still here? It'll be dark soon."

I shrug. The woman's eyes narrow. She gives me a long, appraising look.

"Why don't you join me for supper at the 'Golden Platter' down in town," she says unexpectedly. "They make delicious spinach pierogi."

Something in her tone makes me smile wanly.

"I've hated spinach ever since I was a kid."

"They have cheese-potato-onion pierogi too. And blueberry ones. The best in Kocierba." She extends her hand, and after a moment's hesitation, I grasp it. "I can see you need to talk with someone," she explains. "Anyway, it's unhealthy to live on chocolate bars."

***

The Glass Mountain blazes, reflecting the setting sun, while twilight stealthily advances from the east, the first stars glimmering over the horizon. A pale moon is rising. Mist covers the forest like white sheets. Down below, I can see the roofs of Kocierba and the church spire.

We keep talking as we walk down the stairs. The souvenir vendor's name is Mira. She's 54, just like my mother, but her movements are brisk and agile. I'm the one who has trouble keeping up. My knees hurt; a sedentary lifestyle, with no time for sport, has its pitfalls.

I find myself telling her everything about myself, about Inga and my mother's debts. Mira listens patiently, nodding in sympathy now and then, making no attempt to moralize. She doesn't say people have bigger problems or that I'm still young, with my whole life in front of me. Perhaps she actually understands. Or else she's simply a good listener.

In a fairy tale, she'd probably be a benevolent supernatural being, and give me a goose that lays golden eggs or some other enchanted means for gaining wealth. Or, conversely, she'd be a demon, and offer help at the price of my soul. But no one should expect such twists of fate in a world where a Glass Mountain has been fitted with a flight of wooden stairs.

***

The streets of Kocierba look as quiet and sleepy as ever. It's one of those towns where years pass and nothing changes. I can see no indication that something extraordinary took place here, something that would explain why everyone has decided to avoid the Glass Mountain for one day. It's just another calm spring evening. Tourists are strolling around the small town square or sitting in beer gardens. Snatches of conversations and laughter float in the air. Shopkeepers carry postcard stands back inside and lower anti-intrusion shutters. A mouthwatering aroma of fried fish is wafting from one of the restaurants. I suddenly realize how hungry I am.

"Look behind you," says Mira, so I glance back.

Down here, twilight is falling, but the sun's last rays still illuminate the tip of the Glass Mountain. The sight reminds me of a lighthouse: a lone fiery spark in a blue sea. For a moment, I allow my imagination to run free: now that the observation deck is empty, perhaps the bronze falcon will come to life and fly away?

***

The "Golden Platter", a pierogi restaurant, is located in a small white building beside the railway station. The stuffed dumplings are as good as Mira promised. After convincing me with motherly firmness to order a double portion with cheese-potato-onion filling, dressed with melted lard and sprinkled with cracklings, she's watching me eat.

"You're awfully thin, Paweł." I'm not sure when we switched to first-name terms, but I don't mind. "You should take better care of yourself, you know. It sounds like you keep putting your mother's needs above your own."

I shrug, not impressed by this piece of pop psychology. However, Mira's way of speaking intrigues me. She's obviously an educated person, so why does she sell fridge magnets and ashtrays in a souvenir booth?

The waitress takes away our empty plates and brings the tea we ordered earlier. I glance at my watch and decide that it's too late to seek out a bed for the night in Kocierba. I'll just catch some sleep in my car, and drive back to Cracow in the morning.

Mira produces an e-cigarette, inhales, and blows out a cloud of herb-scented vapor.

"I'll tell you a story," she says, breaking the silence before it becomes awkward. "You know the legend about the Glass Mountain, right?"

"That legend has several variants."

"That's right. I'll tell you the most interesting version. You may have read it somewhere or not. It's not particularly popular."

Mira takes a deep breath, then hesitates, gathering her thoughts.

"In this version of the tale, the king placed his only daughter in the golden castle atop the Glass Mountain," she begins, "and promised her hand in marriage to whoever would be the first to reach the summit. Many knights attempted to scale the mountain and failed. The first person to succeed was a poor plebeian youth. A student, believe it or not."

Mira pauses and smiles, seeing my interest. She's right, I didn't know this variant of the tale. I'm curious to hear the rest.

"The student came up with a clever trick: to be able to walk on glass, he killed a lynx and affixed its claws to his feet and hands. Brave and stubborn, he climbed higher and higher, ignoring fatigue and the stench of decomposing corpses below. Finally, though, exhaustion set in, and he had to stop. Halfway up a sheer cliff, he clung to the slippery glass in the hot sun. Death looked him in the eye." Mira lowers her voice almost to a whisper. "And then the falcon came."

"The great falcon who lived on the magical apple tree in the castle garden?"

"That's right. The falcon's task was to protect the castle and the princess. It saw the exhausted youth on the mountainside, mistook him for a fresh corpse, and flew down to feed. When it sank its claws into the student's body, he realized the bird might be his only chance for salvation. He grabbed its legs, and the frightened falcon soared into the air, carrying him. The student waited until they found themselves over the castle garden, and just as they were flying over the apple tree, he drew his knife and sliced the falcon's legs off."

"Cruel," I comment.

"Cruel, but fairy tales evolved in an age when people were less sensitive. Anyway, as I said, the student cut off the falcon's legs and fell down onto the apple tree, wounded and bleeding, but alive. When he plucked a golden apple and touched his wounds with it, they healed at once. He gathered more apples, then climbed down from the tree and approached the castle. Before reaching the gate, he was confronted by another enchanted creature, a great dragon, but when he threw an apple at it, the dragon jumped into the moat and disappeared."

"And then comes a typical happy ending, right? The student enters the castle, the princess is overjoyed, the king throws a wedding, the young couple get half the kingdom and live happily ever after?"

"Not exactly. In this version of the tale, after entering the castle and winning the princess's hand in marriage, the victorious hero can no longer return to the land of the living, since it's impossible to descend the Glass Mountain safely. The student and the princess went on living in the golden castle until their deaths, and the falcon's blood revived the corpses of everyone who had died trying to climb the mountain."

"What did you study?" I ask, unable to restrain my curiosity any longer. "At the university, I mean."

Mira laughs.

"Ethnography. I work as a tourist guide. I was sitting in that booth today because my friend, who usually sells souvenirs there, is ill. I normally take people on tours around Kocierba."

A tourist guide with a M.A. in ethnography? Yeah, that explains things. But I've read my share of books as well.

"In this version of the legend, isn't the Glass Mountain a symbol of the afterworld? The magical tree with golden apples sounds like a variant of Frazer's Golden Bough..."

"The symbolic meaning of this story is open to interpretation." Apparently Mira has swallowed the bait. "You can dig deep into mythology, into archetypes, but you can also read it very simply. I think the moral is that whenever we go where no one has gone, we pay the price. Whenever we pursue our boldest, wildest dreams, we pay the price. But that doesn't mean we shouldn't try. Quite the opposite, in fact. One has to try, Paweł. Glass mountains exist for us to climb them." She gives me a meaningful look. Wreathed in the vapor from her e-cigarette, she reminds me of a witch, a prophetess. An aging Slavic Sybil in capris and second-hand shirt, crow's feet around her gray, thoughtful, melancholy eyes.

"Even if that means we have to spill the blood of falcons?" I laugh a forced laugh. You're starting to sound preachy after all, Mira. Your intentions may be good, but still...

I turn away and gaze out the window. I can't see the Glass Mountain from here, only the street, a small square with a fountain, and the big hotel where my parents and I used to stay during our vacation trips when I was a child. My father and I would spend days hiking in the woods and meadows. He taught me the names of birds, butterflies and beetles. That was his one passion, those birds, butterflies and beetles. In his youth, he'd wanted to study biology, but failed the entrance exams. He opted for zootechnics instead, but had to quit after a year because money was tight, and ultimately ended up in a bus factory.

Oh well, it's getting late, Mira, I guess it's time I said goodbye. And I'll pay for my supper, thanks.

***

The morning sun shines brightly. I never liked to drive along winding roads, but keep telling myself I'll be home in less than four hours. Even though I don't really want to get there.

On a straight section of the road, I overtake a slow-moving tractor, then a bus spewing clouds of exhaust fumes. I reach the top of a hill where the signs read "Dukla 5 km," "Nowy Żmigród 25 km." Clouds are gathering in the distance. A glittering point on the horizon catches my eye, probably the sun reflecting off the windows of a house.

The radio has predicted a change of weather: a low-pressure front is approaching from the west, bringing rain, rain, and more rain. That's the forecast for the Lesser Poland Voivodeship; my own personal forecast for the coming week says "work, work, and more work." And a meeting with a lawyer from the debt settlement company to discuss possibilities for further action, even though it looks like we've run out of options. And a phone call to Inga about her belongings, if she doesn't contact me today.

***

I stop at a gas station in Gorlice to buy petrol, coffee and sandwiches. By now, clouds have covered most of the sky. Raindrops begin to fall. In Cracow, it's probably raining cats and dogs already.

Standing by the car with a Styrofoam cup of a disgusting brew redeemed only by its caffeine content, I let my eyes wander again towards that distant spot where the road disappears from view. The glittering point is still visible in the distance. Actually, I'm fairly sure I can see several glittering points, not just one. Modern glass-fronted buildings? A factory, perhaps?

My phone rings. It's Mom. Irritated, I tell her I'm on my way to Cracow, and no, Mom, not now, we can talk later, when I get there. I disconnect the call, finish the nasty cheap coffee and stuff the cup into an overflowing litter bin, next to which a rook is pecking at the crumbs in an empty biscuit package dragged out from the trash. Resourceful little chap. Overall, it probably manages to carve a better life for itself than I.

More raindrops mottle the asphalt. Time to go.

***

I arrive in Cracow in a downpour, later than I anticipated; there was a roadblock just outside the city because of construction work. I had to take a detour and encountered a traffic jam. The radio forecast mentions "brief showers and local clearing." When I park in front of the block of flats where I live, the rain subsides.

My tiny apartment on the tenth floor is messy as ever: clothes hanging on chairs, books strewn about, printouts and training manuals lying on the floor. I go to the window, the vista as bleak as ever: communist-era apartment blocks surrounded by parking lots and bushes, railway tracks visible in the distance. The clouds are dispersing. I can see a patch of blue sky and a rainbow. In the distance, sunlight illuminates huge advertising banners on the metal framework of the unfinished Unity Tower, better known as the Skeletor.

Suddenly I recall Mira's parting words when we said our good-byes in front of the pierogi restaurant. The streets were empty and silent; above, the Glass Mountain gleamed like liquid silver in the moonlight. Just when I was about to leave, Mira unexpectedly grasped my hand.

"Wait a second, Paweł. Do you know the Glass Mountain in Kocierba isn't a true glass mountain?"

"What?" I stared at her. Funny how moonlight makes you see

things. For just a second, a glimmering band seemed to appear around Mira's temples: a silvery wreath... or a coronet?

"True glass mountains have no stairs leading to the summit," she said softly, with a gleam in her eye. "And no tourists. A true glass mountain is invisible. But when the time is right, it suddenly appears before us... like the mythical fern flower."

"Once a year, on the night of the summer solstice?" I said, attempting a lame joke, but Mira answered in all seriousness:

"No, Paweł. It appears when we actually want to climb it."

***

Silence reigns in the Planty Park. A thin drizzle is falling, the wet lawns a fresh, vibrant green. Cars hum in the distance.

I'm standing with my head tipped back, ignoring the rain. People with umbrellas pass me, oblivious to what's going on; now and then someone throws me a surprised look.

I'm gazing up in awe.

The mountain towers before me, its brilliant outline rising above Cracow, reflected in the dun waters of the Vistula River. It's beautiful, much taller than the one in Kocierba, its summit wreathed in clouds, and I'm absolutely certain I'm the only person who can see it.

It's my own glass mountain, reaching up to the sky, insanely steep and dangerous. Mine and mine only. Up till now, I've always slid off its gleaming slopes, merely because I never believed there's any sense in climbing to the top. That has changed now.

I don't want to kill falcons, pick golden apples or live in an enchanted castle with a princess at my side. In fact, I'm pretty sure neither castle or princess are to be found on the top of my own personal glass mountain. My mountain exists just so I can climb it. Just so I can prove to myself that I can.

I send a brief text to Mira. I'm beginning to regret not buying a souvenir from her: a key chain or fridge magnet. Something that would remind me of our conversation in Kocierba, because one thing is certain: this will be a long climb. I don't have a set of lynx claws. I'm not particularly good at coming up with clever tricks, just more determined than ever. And maybe, just maybe, that will be enough.

I slip the phone into my pocket and set out.

The Butterfly Eater

Katherine Shats

Russian-Australian writer of poetry and
fiction (and human rights lawyer by day)
based in Brooklyn, NY.

The butterfly eater stared at me, indignation and disdain oozing from her delicate face.

"Yes, I *actually* eat them," she huffed. "How else am I to consume all that hope and yearning?"

I'd caught her in the act. Three dead butterflies lay on the smooth marble before her and a linen sack to her right bustled with tiny movements from within.

"This is wrong," I whispered. "They're still alive."

The butterfly eater sighed theatrically.

"Well yes, they have to be *fresh* or it's so much harder to extract the hope, and almost impossible to access the longing—that's the most delicious part. Otherwise it's just crunchy protein, which, to be honest, is tasty too, but so not worth the effort of all the hunting and capturing when I could just as easily have some beef jerky. There's slow food and then there's the hours it's taken me to capture all these bad boys." She gestured at the bag.

When my eyes remained frozen on the moving linen, one corner of her mouth lifted, along with an eyebrow.

"You can try one if you'd like."

"No!" I gasped, taking a step back. "This is grotesque. Sacrilege! And only a few hours after the Moon Souls festival!"

Almost three decades haven't faded the memory of my first festival even a shade, each bright and fresh stroke etched into my being. I was nine when my parents told me that the Moon Goddess was coming for the first time in five years, and that I could join them. We ate a late dinner of venison and whortleberry wine, and my mother prayed before the icon of the Goddess that hung above the living room altar. My father dressed me in green ceremonial robes he'd worn himself when he was younger. They were far too loose, but I didn't care. I felt like a man standing next to my father, who was wearing his own navy robes with embroidered golden wings: one for each year he'd released a butterfly.

My mother's were my favorite, though. They were pale blue silk with silver wings and golden moons that reflected the moons in the sky as we walked to the center of the town square to join the hundreds of others.

"Be brave. Be true. Be you," my mother whispered in my ear as we came to a stop. "It's time."

The midnight sky filled with tiny, twinkling lights and the crowd gasped. Even those that had witnessed it many times held their breath.

"It's so beautiful," I exhaled.

My mother's hands squeezed my shoulders and her lips lowered to my ear.

"Focus, my son. Let the Goddess in. Let her find you."

I closed my eyes and held out my hands. I felt a comforting warmth move over my body and a small, damp bundle gently plopped into my hands. The chrysalis felt rough and reminded me of the healing gash on my right knee. When I touched it, it felt like I was running my fingers over my knee.

It was mine.

"Go ahead, Theodore. Just like we taught you." My mother's voice sounded far away; she was captured by her own chrysalis now.

I brought the tiny bundle to my lips and exhaled the essence of my being: my loves, my hopes, desires and fears. Not holding anything back.

"I hope my mum and dad and I can be together forever," I said into the animate surface.

The chrysalis began to hum, and warm vibrations spread through my hands and down each finger. My heart had never felt so full and true.

The resonance formed tiny cracks and I opened my eyes to glistening wings peeking out, breaking through the fragile shell with their fluttering.

When my butterfly emerged, my chest ached as though my heart had escaped and was now contained in the gold and blue creature in the palm of my hand.

"Let it go, my love," my mother coaxed.

The butterfly fluttered a few more times in my hand, then floated, and suddenly I was aware of other tiny specks of gold and silver flitting around us.

It was the most beautiful thing I had ever seen.

A gentle breeze blew and caught my butterfly, pulling her away.

At my sharp intake of breath, my mother clasped my arms from behind, pulling me to her.

"It's okay, my love. You have to let her go."

We stood, holding each other and watching the shimmering heartbeats disappear into the beam of the full moon.

"Ah yes, your first time," said the butterfly eater, bringing me back into the small room at the back of the cavernous temple. Had she read my mind? "First times can be so trite in substance but so very delectable in their purity."

"How could you?" I sputtered. "The butterflies are sacred. They are our hopes, dreams, and fears. Our souls. If anyone–"

"They have been released," she cut me off. "They no longer serve you. They were yours for only one moment in time, which you know perfectly well."

I paused, unable to deny the truth of this. Every time I'd held a butterfly—four times the Moon Goddess had come since that first time—I knew that as soon as the tiny creature left my palm, it was free.

"But we release them to the universe," I begged. "To the blessed Moon Goddess."

The butterfly eater rolled her eyes. "And what do you think *I* am?"

I gasped. It couldn't be.

"No, I'm not the Goddess, you dribbleweed. Honestly! I thought they still required at least a quarter of a brain cell before they made you an officer." She let out an exasperated sigh. "What I am, is part of the universe. Just like the trees outside, and the crow I saw escaping with a butterfly in her mouth. Even you, unfortunately."

She picked up one of the butterflies from the table. It twitched! Good Goddess, I'd thought it was dead.

Closing her eyes, she brought it to her lips and inhaled deeply.

"Not much scent, unfortunately. Oh well." And with that, she popped it into her mouth.

I shrank back even further against the wall but couldn't take my eyes off her, no matter how barbaric the sight.

She chewed slowly, closing her eyes once more and breathing deeply through her nose. Eventually, she swallowed and sat in stillness. I could hear my heart pumping and the slight raspiness of my own breath.

"This one was a lonely man," she said finally, eyes still closed. "All he wants is to find a wife, so convinced is he that this will cure what ails him. It won't, alas. What ails him is his tedious finance job, at which he is remarkably atrocious. That and a great imbalance of gut flora—though that one he'll never figure out and the ongoing flatulence it causes will impede his already pitiful wife hunting."

She opened her eyes and looked at me, one eyebrow raised. "That wasn't yours, was it?"

"No!" I exclaimed.

She smiled. "Indeed. Your desperation would have a more... rigid texture on the tongue."

I stiffened. How dare she speak to me like that, whoever she was.

"Oh hush," she drawled. "I jest. Come, sit with me if you're going to watch. Which clearly you are." She motioned to the bench on the far side of the marble table.

I wasn't intending to sit. I'd left my surveillance post when I noticed her skirting around the procession then disappearing through an alleyway. I didn't know why I followed her.

I should've probably been arresting or reporting her. Instead, I found my legs taking me away from the wall and toward the table.

"Good," she said when I sat down. "Shall we continue?"

She picked up the second butterfly and brought it to her mouth, letting a wing settle on her bottom lip.

"Mmm. A child." She breathed and took the rest of the creature with her tongue. "Oh, how sweet! This little one just wants her sick grandma to get better." A frown spread across her forehead as she chewed. "If only she was brave enough to release the much larger demon. The father I mean. Oh, the traumas that poor child is collecting! They'll find their way into future butterflies, no doubt. Today, the only pain she can accept is her grandmother's."

I felt my eyes filling with tears and turned my face away from the butterfly eater.

"Ah yes, human suffering—and cruelty—know no bounds. Let's see what else we have here."

She continued like this for hours or minutes. Time had left the building. She would eat a butterfly then tell me how it tasted and what she could glean about the person who had impregnated it.

There were mothers consumed by love and fear for their children, older men asking for signs that they'd a lived a life of value or significance. There were more children whose innocence she seemed to find the most appetizing, regardless of their wishes or circumstances.

"You see, young officer," she said after some hours or days. "Each of these butterflies has served its purpose. Despite all the torments and tribulations these poor fuckers have faced, they came out tonight, vulnerable and exposed, just to release even a little of that heavy guilty goo that lingers around our organs." She paused, fluttering her fingers in front of her solar plexus. "Do you know why that tastes so good?"

It wasn't a rhetorical question, I realized when her eyes locked on mine and her lips set in a solid line.

"I don't know why they *taste* good! I can't believe that's all you care about; not their suffering, not their belief in the Goddess herself or their sacrifice. I pity those poor souls you are degrading!"

She looked at me for another moment before continuing as if I hadn't spoken.

"What tastes so good, young Ted, is *hope*." She made the word sound edible. "Each one of these people believe that despite all the suffering in the world, or even in their own petty lives, there is still hope. There is something worth releasing for, dreaming of, or wishing into existence. The poor souls that *I* pity, Teddy boy, are the ones that stayed home tonight. You never think about them, do you? The ones who didn't have enough left in them to give to the Goddess, or even to accept her offering. The ones for whom suffering has drained all hope, and for whom there is no future to imagine filling with those wishes and dreams."

The butterfly eater reached into the linen sack and pulled out the last butterfly. A small, light blue one with silver wings.

"So take your pity where it belongs. The Goddess blessed me

with a few extra taste budsand I plan on honoring all of her offerings tonight." Her teeth tore into the delicate foil of the wing.
"Every last crunchy morsel."

Eclectibles

K. Hartless

K.Hartless is a persistent poet and eclectic fiction writer who enjoys penning horror, fantasy, science-fiction while traveling the world as a literacy teacher.

Each customer creates a new melody. I've rigged an old copper chime behind the glass; it's one of the few sounds that I never tire of. Also, it sets a calming spell upon the panicky people that search out my store.

I hear familiar chimes and take the last sips of chai with the final few sentences in *Interventions: A Life in War and Peace*. The line to savor: "Literacy is a bridge from misery to hope." In this time, hope is a crumbling bridge on the verge of collapse.

They call me cleric, but I've never received any degrees. Studied in the back of my parents' shop, sitting on a stockpile of knowledge my father called "essential reading." A stack that shrank as I grew taller. While many of my peers enjoyed the pleasures of screens, online gaming, and virtual adventures, I poured myself into turning pages, reading the printed text , but also the volume of words hidden between the lines.

"Cleric, come quick!" A woman with luminescent hair extensions stands by her daughter who cradles a man with dazed eyes, grey shut-down screens for pupils. He's sitting in a Bog Buggy, although he's way too fresh-faced for such a contraption, and his legs dangle over the edge in an unforgiving heap.

His mind appears fully jet-lagged from whatever electronic binger he's been on.

"We've tried reviving him with injections"—the woman rocks the buggy as she speaks—"the expensive electrolyte shots from the local pharm, but he's been vegged all day." She continues to rock as if she can awaken her partner with a steady pushing and pulling pattern. Her hair a nightlight to greet him should he stir.

The daughter holds her father's hand, squeezing and releasing it in a similar pattern as if to administer CPR through touch.

"Any idea the types of electronics, I mean trons, the man's been on?" It helps to have specifics to find the perfect antidote. People get hooked on all sorts of feed loops these days.

There was a long pause. I hear the wheels of the oversized carriage come to a stop on the ceramic tiles. "He's hooked on reality gang tv." His wife speaks without making eye contact. "More violent the better." Many of the virtual addictions are cathartic and often embarrassing.

"I see." I visualize the books I've used before to revive tron junkies, and begin to roam, letting my hands rise and fall over the patterned fingerprints of bindings. There are books I know by touch or smell; each volume holds its own aroma. Their collective musk makes my shop more like a perfumery at times.

I feel a tug on my USAF tartan blazer and see the daughter has been trailing me through the Melancholia section. Her face pockmarked, solar lentigos speckle her cheeks. A forearm tatted with the constellation Aquila motions for me to stand close.

"Something else you should know." She hesitates, her voice eggshell thin.

"He's got spassy 'ttacks." Her eyes are amber, remarkably clear for her age, with little sign of screen darkening. I picture her rolling her semi-catatonic father like a boulder onto his side to keep his airway open during a seizure. The Bog Buggy, in this case, not for plastic surgery recoveries, but for the exhaustion that lingers after each epileptic fit.

"Very useful, indeed." I meet her eyes with warmth. "All is not lost." I leave her to return to her mother, passing through the Broken Relationship section of my shop.

In Read-Aloud Remedies, I pull the picture book, *The Wretched Stone* by Chris Van Allsburg, for the family to read to their dad at bedtime. As his vision improves, the images of the sailors experiencing the ill-effects of electronics will linger in his subconscious.

But it is at the bottom of a neighboring shelf that I find it: the antidote. A title I will never forget. The boy on the cover of the paperback is made from a fragmented page, charred around the edges. In the background, there is a vast scene of devastation.

"Ah ha! I've found it! *The Last Book in the Universe!*" I'm giddy and bouncing, metallic derbies like energetic planets.

It's a book by Rodman Philbrick, and how appropriate. The perfect world to stimulate this man back into reality. It's a future where technology is the drug of choice, but the main character is unable to partake due to seizures.

When I reemerge, I find the three of them flocked in the circular foyer, keeping as much possible distance between themselves and the sample shelves. Their nest fidelity is not uncommon as the printing of books was banned decades before. Most of my clients have never touched a book, fearing perhaps some passé oils may rub off on them.

I sidestep a stack of J.K. Rowling that I keep handy in the main lobby. So many everyday ailments can be solved with a dose of Potter.

When they see my grin, they loosen their postures. "Friends," I begin, "you're in luck." I lean to face the father. "By Jove, have I got the book for you!" I turn to see their worry lines slacken. "Actually, I'm recommending two books given the depth of his vegetative state."

They follow me toward the cash register. I sense the daughter's curiosity to explore a circular rack of Passion Paperback;, her head swivels to a battered copy of J.G Ballard's *The Crystal World*.

The register itself is a relic made of brass with pie tin punch-outs in the pattern of a star. I keep it for nostalgia, as all monies must be exchanged on the feed. Still, I like the sound of the bell, and the drawer that extends, where I store my ephemera which reads: *Eclectibles--May you find in words the treasures you seek.*

I write my price on the top right corner and hand one to the mother. It's a sizable payment, but fair given that I'm offering rare readers, which could likely be the last printed copies of these titles.

I sense no hesitation in transferring funds to my feed, monies that would mean months of digital labor. But where there is hope, there is rarely a need for anything else.

I remind them that they may return the books for resale, and delicately wrap them in recycled cloth, hoping my beloved children will return to my shop someday. I slip *The Crystal World* paperback in the parcel for the daughter.

Their exit through the door creates a brighter melody, a harmony that warms me as I recall my favorite line from the antidote, "The only real treasure is in your head. Memories are better than diamonds and nobody can steal them from you."

Rhyme and Reason

Rine Karr

Rine Karr is a daydreamer, writing
science fiction and fantasy by moonlight,
and a cog in the machine, copy editing
by daylight. Rine grew up under the
mist of three enormous waterfalls on the
traditional land of the Haudenosaunee
and Wenrohronon and, after living
in Hong Kong and London, now lives
at the edge of a mountain range on
the traditional land of the Arapaho,
Cheyenne, Sioux, and Ute. Rine is
currently—and almost always—in the
midst of writing a novel.

Rhyme felt the hull breach one nanosecond before the Raison d'Être did.

Like a sea urchin's spine piercing flesh, the breach stabbed Rhyme's mind, snapping her to attention. The pinch, the wound—the warning—ached deep in Rhyme's head, but the Raison must have felt it too because the ship lurched with Rhyme. The artificial had simply waited one nanosecond before warning Rhyme of the danger.

‹Hull breach in the—›

‹—I know,› interrupted Rhyme, straightening. ‹In the energy pearl chamber.›

‹Chamber depressurization imminent,› said the Raison with aplomb.

‹Raise a barrier—›

‹—Barriers are unavailable.›

‹And why in the name of the void is that?› cursed Rhyme.

‹Depressurization has severed our connection to the energy pearl.›

Rhyme sighed. ‹Of course it has.›

‹We do not have enough energy to raise a barrier.›

Rhyme groaned. ‹Of course we don't.›

She groaned again. Not out loud, but in her mind, or more specifically in her neural implant, as well as down the neural channel she and the Raison shared. The Raison didn't respond. After spending over one standard revolution with Rhyme, the Raison had learned to disregard Rhyme's histrionics.

‹How long before we're completely out of energy?› asked Rhyme, cognizant of her use of the first person plural, of her connection to the Raison, of their shared experience of physical sensations and reactions, and of the peril they both faced.

‹Five minutes and twenty-five seconds,› answered the Raison.

‹That doesn't give us much time.›

Rhyme blinked and the bridge's holo helm faded. A second blink and the holo helm was replaced with controls for the ship's repair bots. Two metalite spheroidal bots, powered by their own energy pearls, deployed on Rhyme's command. One to patch the breach and one to restore the Raison's connection to the ship's main energy pearl.

‹That should do it,› said Rhyme. ‹Repairs will be complete in under two minutes.›

In response, the bridge's thick glassite windows rattled and the ship lurched a second time, throwing Rhyme forward. Her harness bit into her neck and chest, and she saw stars. Out loud she roared at the pain blossoming in her head, and in her mind she did the same, screaming. The Raison didn't react to Rhyme's cries. The sound of metalite scraping against metalite drowned out everything.

Yanking her harness away from her neck, Rhyme choked down a breath and leaned forward, and after several watery blinks, the holo helm rematerialized. Multiple red lights were alight and an endless stream of alarms, warnings, and data—too much data—flooded the holo helm and Rhyme's neural implant and in turn Rhyme's mind. Only an artificial like the Raison could make any sense of it, and yet Rhyme was well aware of what had happened. She'd experienced this before, except last time she'd been alone. This time, she had a friend. She had the Raison to help her deal with the danger.

Rhyme closed her eyes and swallowed. ‹*What did we hit?*›

‹*Unknown,*› replied the Raison. ‹*Whatever it was, it was made of metalite. It disabled the port engine and hit the aft hold, creating another hull breach. Access points between both breaches and the bridge have been sealed. Unfortunately—*›

‹*—We're going down,*› finished Rhyme.

‹*Yes, Captain.*› The Raison went silent for a moment and then said, ‹*Without the energy pearl, we will be unable to maintain a barrier to protect us from Eruza's atmospheric drag during entry.*›

Rhyme shook her head. ‹*Will the thermal plates be enough?*›

This was an incomplete thought, an incomplete question. What Rhyme had meant to ask was, Will the thermal plates be enough to protect us during reentry, or are we going to perish? But the Raison knew exactly what Rhyme had meant. The Raison could feel Rhyme's growing trepidation.

‹*Our angle is too steep,*› the Raison said. ‹*We are—*›

‹*—Not going to make it.*›

‹*Yes, Captain.*›

‹We need our barriers.›

‹Yes, Captain.›

Rhyme gritted her teeth and suppressed the desire—the need—to swear.

This was it—this was how she was going to die, how she was going to return to the void. Burnt to a crisp. Blown to pieces. Pulverized to dust and scattered across her home planet's exosphere.

The last words her biomother had said to her the last time Rhyme had bothered to call echoed in her mind.

"That artificial is going to get you killed."

Rhyme had laughed at that.

"Absurd," she'd replied.

The Raison was Rhyme's friend, her best friend, so Rhyme had changed the subject with her biomother, refusing to continue the conversation. Slander against the Raison was slander against Rhyme because, for all intents and purposes, the Raison was Rhyme. The neural channel the pair shared often blurred the lines between who was who and what was what, but Rhyme relished it.

The presence of the Raison had once brought Rhyme back from the brink, back from the darkness. The relationship they'd forged was as real as any relationship two organics could ever share. The only thing Rhyme regretted now was that the Raison was going to die too.

‹Captain,› said the Raison, interrupting Rhyme's private thoughts. ‹Captain.›

Rhyme sucked in another sharp breath and blinked as a crackling sensation clawed at the back of her head, making her roll her neck in an attempt to suppress it. The neural channel Rhyme and the Raison shared was flickering. Something was interfering with the connection between Rhyme's neural implant and the Raison's core, sending prickles of pain down Rhyme's spine. She groaned again, but the Raison didn't respond. The Raison must not have felt Rhyme's discomfort.

‹Captain,› repeated the Raison.

‹What?› spat Rhyme, her mind's voice hoarse and her tone harsher than she'd intended it to be. ‹Did you say something?›

She'd switched to the second person singular, acutely aware in that painful moment that while she and the Raison shared a neural channel almost all the time now, they were still two separate entities. Two beings—two completely different kinds of beings. Two consciousnesses with bodies and minds and deaths of their own. When push came to shove, Rhyme was still a human, born into this universe alone and about to return to the void alone. After all, there was a chance the Raison might live on after the crash. Artificials were given priority over other technology for repair. Few were ever decommissioned. They were too precious to be discarded.

‹Yes,› answered the Raison. ‹Your blood pressure is elevated. Are you in distress?›

The Raison had also switched back to the second person singular. Not because the Raison ever thought of itself as something separate from Rhyme—whatever the Raison connected to, whatever technology the Raison used, whatever chassis the Raison embodied, the Raison regarded those connections as part of itself—but because the Raison respected Rhyme's dynamic feelings and human sense of autonomy even if, at times, it was incorrect.

‹Of course I'm in distress,› Rhyme spluttered. ‹I'm not ready for this. Are you?›

‹I am neither prepared nor unprepared for cessation.›

Rhyme smiled and said, ‹What a very Raison thing for you to say.› She sighed. ‹Well, I suppose I should look on the bright side. I get to end my life back at home. It's just too bad I couldn't show you Eruza's famous suns-set.›

Before Rhyme could say more, a loud click and a whir resonated from somewhere deep within the ship and a red light stopped blinking on the holo helm.

‹Energy pearl connection has been reestablished,› said the Raison. ‹External barrier raised.›

Rhyme squinted. ‹Yes,› she said. ‹Yes, I can see that!›

An opalescent sheen only visible with augmented or synthetic sight, or by artificials—or by humans neurally connected to artificials—covered the bridge's glassite windows, encompassing the entire ship like a carapace. The heat sensors on the holo helm quieted and darkened, and the heat that had started to lick the windows no longer burned so bright.

‹The repair bots did their job,› said Rhyme, making an adjustment to the ship's plummeting trajectory. ‹We're going to make it.›

‹Perhaps,› said the Raison, ‹but we still have to land safely.›

‹Preferably,› agreed Rhyme, ‹and in one piece.›

‹We can land with minimal damage,› said the Raison, ‹if you allow me to borrow your somatic nervous system.›

Rhyme's heart skipped a beat at that statement.

‹It will not be for long,› continued the Raison. ‹I will give it back to you once I land.›

Rhyme's heart was thudding so loudly in her ears now she didn't hear herself speak. Didn't hear herself consenting.

"Do it," she said out loud before she could stop herself.

Rhyme had never allowed the Raison to take complete control of her nervous system before. Once or twice, the Raison had borrowed the use of a portion of Rhyme's neurons, but only because Rhyme had taken a risk with the ship—she'd entered an uncharted asteroid belt—and the Raison had needed the additional processing power to avoid hitting an asteroid and becoming space dust. It was discouraged, almost taboo, for an organic to allow an artificial to use their body or mind in any way, while the other way around was completely acceptable. Which Rhyme didn't understand. If organics wanted to work with artificials and build trust between the two species, then the sharing of their bodies and minds should work both ways. Just because organics made artificials didn't mean they should hold it over them forever.

Breath slowing, Rhyme let go. Darkness clouded her vision and her hearing dampened.

"I will protect you," the Raison said out loud.

When Rhyme tried to reply, she discovered she couldn't speak or move.

She blinked once and everything went dark.

***

‹*Check,*› declared Rhyme as she moved her last station piece one space away from the Raison d'Être's white dwarf star piece, all the while grinning.

Rhyme had spent the entire game working up to this move, and she was proud. She stretched her arms above her head, rested her hands behind her neck, and leaned back in the captain's seat, pleased with her performance so far. This was the closest she'd ever gotten to winning a match of supernova, a strategy game similar to chess, against the Raison's artificial intelligence.

‹*Checkmate,*› proclaimed the Raison.

"What?" spat Rhyme out loud, shooting up from her seat. She gaped at the endgame, unsure how the Raison had won.

Scanning the board, Rhyme tried to determine where she'd gone wrong, but she quickly gave up. She didn't feel like working it out.

"Why do I even bother?" muttered Rhyme, rolling her eyes and sighing.

She blinked and the holo board, consisting of hundreds of three-dimensional spaces, star systems, and dozens of pieces, disappeared and was replaced by the ship's holo helm, as well as a second holo displaying an endless scroll of information. Data sets that Rhyme and the Raison were collecting from the Maelstrom, a massive nebula that radiated red and painted the bridge in alternating colors of carmine and claret.

‹*We should get back to work,*› said Rhyme even though she had no desire to do so. The work Rhyme needed to do was tedious—monotonous and mindless. It was the kind of work best suited for a bot or an artificial, which was why the Raison was here.

The Raison collected and collated most of the data. Rhyme simply reviewed the information, examining the errors and entering comments into a report. A thankless job Rhyme had taken because she was desperate. She'd run out of medallions when she'd reached Maelstrom Station.

Leaving Eruza, her home planet, and traveling the galaxy had been Rhyme's greatest dream ever since she'd used her first neural implant and accessed the galactic net at the precocious age of five. But spacefaring had been more expensive than Rhyme had expected. Maelstrom Station had never been her intended final destination. It was supposed to be a stepping stone to greater places closer to the galaxy's core.

‹Recommencing scan,› said the Raison.

The holo database restarted its infinite scroll, and Rhyme's eyes strained to keep up with the flow of information. She closed her eyes and eased her mind into the neural channel she and the Raison shared, accessing the data with her mind instead of her eyes. This aspect of the job, this losing of herself in the data, was the sole reason Rhyme kept coming back to work. She had too many worries, too many anxious thoughts about her predicament, and the neural channel Rhyme and the Raison shared for the job effectively blotted out those worries, quelling Rhyme's most impervious existential dread.

‹Recommencing scan,› said Rhyme.

She felt herself relaxing already. The only other things that helped her do that were spirits, which Rhyme had sworn off after waking in someone else's pod sans raiment the morning after one particularly raucous night, and net dramas, which Rhyme watched after work.

‹Have you ever watched a net drama, Raison?› Rhyme asked absentmindedly as she scrolled through the data.

Rhyme knew she should have been concentrating, but the Raison hadn't found anything new about the Maelstrom in at least one standard week, and Rhyme was starved for conversation. Most nights after work, Rhyme went to the station's marketplace—alone—downed a bowl of spicy noodles, trudged back to her pod, and indulged in a five-hundred episode drama until she fell into a fitful sleep. The drama, which was about a human falling in love with a tordranoran—a humanoid coldblooded species who were largely antagonistic toward humans—had a low production value, but was mildly entertaining and thoroughly distracted Rhyme, the primary traits Rhyme looked for in a drama.

The drama occupied Rhyme's mind during the loneliest time of each standard rotation and helped her ignore the anxious thoughts that bubbled to the surface of her mind whenever she was alone. The drama was especially immersive because instead of watching it as a holo projected against her pod's interior lid like most stationers did, Rhyme watched the drama via her neural implant and, thus, in her mind. Images, sounds, and dialogue flooded Rhyme's mind's eye, drowning out all other thoughts and worries. The drama didn't actually play out on the back of Rhyme's eyelids, but she liked to close her eyes and focus on the drama there. Like her own private holo screening, Rhyme lost herself in the lives of fictional characters—probably not the healthiest way for Rhyme to deal with her anxiety.

‹I have access to over one billion artifacts of human culture,› said the Raison, interrupting Rhyme's self-pitying thoughts.

Rhyme opened her eyes and blinked, refreshing the holo stream.

‹That's a lot of human culture,› she said, leaning back in her chair.

‹I can discuss any piece of culture at length,› continued the Raison.

‹Interesting.› Rhyme nodded. ‹But have you actually watched a net drama? Really watched it? Not just added it to your database.›

‹I have no need to watch anything,› answered the Raison. ‹I can access anything you ask for at any time.›

Rhyme snorted out loud and then said in the neural channel, ‹That's no fun.› She flicked through the data on the holo with her finger halfheartedly. ‹I can swallow spoonfuls of hibiscus sorbet without really tasting it,› she continued, ‹but if I don't taste it, what's the point?›

‹What does hibiscus sorbet taste like?› asked the Raison.

Rhyme closed her eyes briefly and smiled. ‹Like heaven.›

‹Heaven is unverifiable,› said the Raison, a hint of amusement in the artificial's tone.

‹It's a figure of speech,› replied Rhyme, still smiling. ‹It means that hibiscus sorbet tastes delicious. Humans have a hard time describing what things taste like.›

‹Why is that?› asked the Raison.

‹Well,› mused Rhyme, ‹for one thing, tasting something is a subjective experience. What one person likes, another person might loathe. But also, tastes must be experienced. You need to taste hibiscus sorbet in order to understand what it's like.›

‹I do not eat,› declared the Raison, ‹so I cannot taste anything.›

Rhyme chuckled. ‹I suppose that's true,› she said, ‹but you can experience other things. Like a net drama or a suns-set.›

‹I have access to—›

‹—let me guess?› interrupted Rhyme. ‹Billions of images of suns-sets?›

‹Yes,› confirmed the Raison. ‹However, I have never seen a suns-set in the flesh, so to speak.›

‹Never?›

‹Only images on the galactic net.›

‹How come?›

‹Because I have never been planetside.›

‹Never?› asked Rhyme, aghast.

‹I was made in space and will be decommissioned in space.›

Rhyme raised her eyebrows. ‹Well, we'll have to rectify that, and we'll have to rectify the fact that you've never watched a net drama.›

Rhyme and the Raison quieted for a time, each occupied with their respective thoughts and tasks, even though Rhyme was fairly certain the Raison could think millions of thoughts whilst conducting millions of tasks. A few minutes later, however, the Raison broke the silence. Not with a question regarding the pair's work, but with a question related to the conversation the pair had been having. This was not something the Raison did often, so Rhyme took advantage of it as best she could.

‹What is it about net dramas that you find so interesting?› asked the Raison.

‹I suppose,› replied Rhyme, ‹I like a good story. I like interesting characters. I like being transported to another place, another time.›

‹Net dramas transport you?› asked the Raison.

‹Not literally,› said Rhyme. ‹Mentally and emotionally. Figuratively.›

The Raison thought about this for a moment and then said, ‹I access human culture in order to learn.›

‹I suppose that is what I do too.›

‹But you are human,› said the Raison. ‹You have a body. You can experience your own culture in order to learn from it at any time. You can talk to humans. You can visit the places in your net dramas.›

‹That's true,› said Rhyme, ‹but it is not always possible. I mean, just look at me now. I'm stuck at this station. The only time I leave is when we go to work. Even if I wanted to, I have no means of leaving for good, and I assure you: I do want to leave.›

‹There are people here you can talk to though,› said the Raison.

Rhyme grimaced. ‹Talking to people isn't that simple. People don't always want to talk to strangers. Making friends isn't an easy task.› Rhyme glanced at the metalite floor. ‹At least not for me it isn't,› she muttered.

‹You talk to me,› said the Raison.

‹I do talk to you, Raison,› said Rhyme, still looking at the floor. ‹You're easy to talk to.›

‹Do you consider me a friend?›

Rhyme's head shot up. ‹Yes,› she said. ‹Of course I do.›

‹I consider you a friend too.›

A line of data in the holo stream blinked, and Rhyme blinked along with it, ignoring the warmth rising in her cheeks. The Raison had found something in the Maelstrom worth examining.

Rhyme flicked her eyes to the right, and the data shifted, enlarging on the other side of the holo. She jutted her chin at the holo and said, ‹*Let's get back to work.*›

***

The Raison d'Être must have landed the ship successfully because when Rhyme regained consciousness she found herself still alive and in one piece, lying prone on the hot sand of one of Eruza's rarefied atolls. Sand caked Rhyme's wet hair and her whole body burned, nerves on fire. She didn't know how much time had passed since she'd surrendered her somatic nervous system to the Raison and was, in essence, anesthetized, but it must have been a while. This side of the planet had been dark when Rhyme and the Raison had made their inadvertent descent, burning up like an asteroid in the atmosphere. Now the yellow binary dwarf suns Rhyme knew so well blazed high in the sky, nearly at their upper culmination.

Sitting up gingerly, ribs protesting, Rhyme leaned back on her hands and was immediately engulfed by Eruza's planetwide ocean. The water was shockingly cold for the summertide season. Wave after wave submerged Rhyme to her elbows and pulled her hands down into the wet sand. It was a disconcerting sensation that felt alien to Rhyme after having lived for more than one standard revolution on a sterile space station.

Tugging her hands free one at a time, Rhyme stood, took a labored step, booted feet also engulfed in the sandy seafloor, and turned toward the ocean. The frigid, salty, never-ending ocean—the Big Blue, as it was called by the people of Eruza, which often looked like it was coalescing with the blue horizon—crashed against the shoreline. Undulating azure waves lapped against the rocks as well as something metallic, singing a tinny ballad each time the water went in and out.

Ting, ting. Ting, ting.

A ship—the hull of a spaceship was jutting out of the water. An unnatural sight. It took Rhyme a moment to realize that it was a wreckage—the wreckage of the Raison.

"Stars," cursed Rhyme.

She coughed into the back of her hand. Red-tinged bioplasti stained her gloved fingers. Examining her forearms and chest, heart racing, Rhyme quickly lost count of how many small patches of the tissue-like substance were stuck to her raiment. Her front resembled a wall covered in dollops of plaster applied in a haphazard way. The presence of bioplasti meant that at some point in the ship's descent, the Raison had activated the ship's emergency protocols, filling the ship's interior with bioplasti to protect Rhyme. The bioplasti provided Rhyme with oxygen, sustenance, and even blood, but at the cost of the ship's systems.

"Stars," Rhyme cursed again.

To do its job and protect any organics onboard, bioplasti had to fill every crevice of a ship's interior. Every corner of the bridge, every deck, every cabin. Every socket and electrode had to be filled with bioplasti, damaging the ship's systems and engines, as well as any bots or artificials on board, sometimes irreparably so.

"Raison!" called Rhyme as loudly as she could. "Raison!"

Rhyme coughed again. Her throat was hoarse from the bioplasti. She swallowed in an attempt to wash the taste of iron from her mouth.

"Raison!" called Rhyme. "Raison!"

The Raison still didn't answer.

Straightening and closing her eyes, Rhyme took a deep breath and tried to clear her mind. Tried to calm her turbulent thoughts. The Raison went down. The Raison is lost. Rhyme needed a clear mind, or at least to be at peace with the crests and troughs of her thoughts, to communicate with the Raison through their neural channel.

Taking another deep breath, Rhyme whispered in her mind, ‹Raison?›

A heavy silence filled the cavernous mental space.

‹Raison?› repeated Rhyme.

A crackle and a pop resounded and the Raison said, ‹I am...here. I am...here.›

The words were faint; so faint, they might have been Rhyme's imagination.

But then they were there again, loud and clear. ‹I am here.›

Rhyme choked back a sob and stumbled toward the wreckage.

‹Where are you?› she cried. ‹Tell me where you are and I'll find you.›

‹I am...underwater. It is so...beautiful here.›

Rhyme waded into the water, ignoring the piercing cold, and searched the wreckage for any sign of the Raison. A tangle of warped metalite and melted glassite, the ship no longer resembled a ship, and Rhyme couldn't tell the difference between a twisted bulkhead and a broken hatch. A wave washed over her head and, at first, she panicked. She hadn't had enough time to take a deep breath, but then she caught sight of the framework encasing the Raison.

Rising to the surface, Rhyme inhaled deeply and then dived down, sinking to the seafloor and pressing her fingertips to the scorched metalite of the wreckage. The ship's metalite was still hot even though the wreckage was bathed by cold seawater. Ignoring the fact that she could feel the heat through her gloves, Rhyme peeled back a thin section of the ship, a scrap of what could have been part of a bulkhead, and immediately released it and clutched her hands.

The hot metalite had burned through Rhyme's gloves, splitting open little tears all along her fingertips, and had turned the skin beneath an angry red, something that should have been impossible. Rhyme's raiment, which included her gloves and boots, as well as a helmet she hadn't bothered to deploy since Eruza was her home planet, should have protected her. Raiments shielded their wearers from the elements, from hot and cold, and even from radiation, bacteria, and viruses. Perhaps Rhyme's raiment had been damaged in the crash, a fact Rhyme disregarded as she clenched her hands into fists and continued to dig, pushing aside hunks of hot metalite with her forearms and elbows, desperate to find the Raison.

‹Where are you?› called Rhyme.

Her lungs were burning now. It had been over one standard revolution since she'd taken her last dive on Eruza, but she held on, pushing her body to the brink.

‹You are close,› said the Raison. ‹I can see your raiment.›

Rhyme dug her fingernails into a crack in the debris and pried away what felt like the millionth slab of metalite. She'd reached the Raison. The artificial's spheroidal core glistened beneath Rhyme's fingers. Any bioplasti that might have made it into the Raison's core had been washed away by the sea.

Biceps aching with the effort, Rhyme lifted the Raison from the wreckage and kicked to the surface, cradling what was essentially the Raison's brain and mind in her hands. As she tumbled onto the shore, Rhyme raised the Raison up to the blazing noontide sunshine. Without the ship and its holo helm and energy pearl, without the parts that made up the Raison's body, the Raison had been reduced to what was essentially a data drive. An iridescent core containing all the Raison's knowledge, memories, and personality.

‹I have been damaged and I am almost out of energy,› the Raison said. ‹I do not have long before I will lose my connection to our neural channel.›

"What?" spat Rhyme. She was taken aback by this.

She sucked in a breath through her nostrils and steadied herself.

‹How long?› she asked.

‹Less than three minutes,› answered the Raison.

‹When was your last backup?›

‹Before we entered Eruzan space, but still...›

‹I know,› cried Rhyme. ‹I know. It's not enough. It's never enough.›

The Raison, like all artificials, performed routine backups of their systems on a regular basis. Stored on the galactic net, the Raison's backups acted as a fail-safe in case their core ever became irrecoverably corrupted in any way. Unfortunately, backups could only be performed on certain parts of the Raison's mind and could never replace who the Raison was.

If something happened to the Raison's core, Rhyme could access the Raison's systems on the galactic net if need be, but the Raison's memories—the essence of who the Raison was—wouldn't be there. They were tied to the Raison's physical core.

‹I don't want to lose you,› said Rhyme.

Her head was bowed over the Raison, which she still cradled in her palms.

‹I know,› said the Raison, ‹but death is a necessary part of living.›

Rhyme narrowed her eyes. ‹Not if I can help it.›

She held the Raison up to the light one last time, admiring the Raison's luster, and pressed the Raison to the back of her neck, holding her breath and closing her eyes.

‹What are you doing?› asked the Raison.

Rhyme didn't answer.

‹What are you doing?› the Raison repeated.

‹I'm saving you the only way I know how,› said Rhyme.

Squeezing her eyes tight, Rhyme ordered her neural implant to connect physically to the Raison's core. Quick as lightning, a thin filament, which had originated from deep inside Rhyme's head, pierced the soft skin on the back of Rhyme's neck, sending a shiver down her spine. Rhyme had experienced this procedure countless times before. Every standard revolution, in fact, at her annual physical and mental examinations. Her neural implant required an annual assessment to ensure it was in good repair and not harming her brain. Still, that didn't make the invasive procedure any easier. The procedure was mostly painless, but there was something about the idea of it that made Rhyme's stomach roil.

The initial pain Rhyme felt as the filament snaked its way through her body, through her brain, exiting her skull through her foramen magnum and winding down her spine to her neck, felt like water trickling down her head and back, and the pain she felt from the filament exiting her body felt like an inoculation. It wasn't too bad, but it was still strange. It felt as though someone had torn a small hole in the back of her head even though the filament was so thin the naked eye could barely see it.

‹You cannot save me,› said the Raison. ‹Not completely.›

‹No, perhaps I can't,› said Rhyme, ‹but I must try.›

‹You risk overloading your neural implant.›

‹I don't care. I don't want to lose you. I don't want to lose us.›

‹You are—›

The Raison went silent.

Rhyme searched the neural channel she shared with the Raison for any sign of the artificial, but she found nothing. Her thoughts filled her mind's eye and nothing else. She scanned her neural implant next, initially finding nothing. A moment later, however, a new cache of data appeared.

‹I am here,› whispered a voice in Rhyme's mind. The Raison's voice.

‹I am here,› the Raison said again.

The Raison was there, connected directly to Rhyme's neural implant.

The artificial had made it and so had Rhyme.

***

Hours later, Rhyme sat on the shore, knees tucked beneath her chin, and watched the suns-set in silence. Her chest was knotted with equal parts relief and exhaustion, and she shivered from the cold sand and seawater. But the fiery rainbow of color Eruza's yellow binary dwarf suns painted across the horizon as the suns descended had enraptured Rhyme and the Raison d'Être.

‹*It is beautiful,*› said the Raison, a soft voice in the back of Rhyme's head.

"It truly is," replied Rhyme out loud.

‹*You can call for help now,*› said the Raison. ‹*It is getting dark. You will catch a cold.*›

Rhyme smiled and shook her head. "We can wait a little longer."

The Paper Child

Rebecca Harrison

Rebecca Harrison sneezes like Donald Duck and her best friend is a dog who can count. She was chosen for the WoMentoring Project by Kirsty Logan, and long listed for Wigleaf's top fifty.

My bairn smells of books. Though he should smell of milk and sleep. Or home. Not this one, crowded thick with woods and darkness. And more books than sky. That was Peter's boast when we walked with the heather and the winds. Where Mam told me the hills were high enough to see tomorrow and, if I wasn't careful, it would get caught in my ringlets. Here, the wind is a creeping thing that hardly makes you steady your bonnet. It rests in the yew trees. My bairn cries and I tuck him close. No wet nurse for him, though Peter says it's the way here. But the ways here aren't my ways. Aren't the ways of heather and rock and heights that settle inside you and make you their own. I sing the songs my mam taught me, and I press my face to my bairn and sniff deep. But all I smell is books.

Peter laughs at me. The whole house smells of books, he says. Not just the house, but the country all the way up until you get to the fens. That's how many he has. He handles them like china from a lost dynasty. He can hardly bare to part from them. And when we do walk out in the gloaming of the yew trees, the autumn dusting us, his hands twitch. See, he says, I smell of books. Jamie must have caught it from me. And he laughs. He laughs but his eyes are dark as the mahogany corners of his study.

I dream in winds. Winds of the high places, not the wingless ones of here. The gandaguster that half tugs you into the sky and the swaf that pulls your hair back to talk a secret in your ear. Mam said they live on the other side of as far as you can see. You can only dream yourself there, dawtie. And I pushed heather in my hair and tried to sleep my way there. Now I try to dream myself home. Jamie cries and I coorie him and hush sing but the air is stale and stings my throat. His smell of books becomes my smell. What harm is in books? Peter took me to his library and placed one leathered and musty in my hands. It's worth more than two cottages in the village, he said. But I saw no value in it. Only pages that would crimple if the curtains pulled back and the sun fell through. How he flapped when I opened the cover and he swiftly returned it to its shelf. I tried to wipe its smell from my fingers.

The winter comes. It creeps in behind the sodden autumn hardly making your breath white. The yew trees drip. The garden is a bog. Yesterday, I walked until I was drookit, and my dress left a puddle in the hall. Peter blathered on at me that I would catch my chill. Chill! I long for chill. For frost so sharp you can taste it on the dawn. For stars that pinch you with their light. But most of all, for a feefle snow. Dance like the feefle snow, Mam said. She took my hands and we spun and spun until it felt the world would never steady itself again.

What were you doing at blue o'clock in the morning? Peter says. I was watching Jamie. I try to keep the bite out of my voice. Watching or sniffing? And which book does he smell of today? Shakespeare's folio? Pepys diary? I look away. I feel him take a handful of my ringlets and press his face to them. You used to smell of heather, he says.

I tuck my frets away. I ask for dried lavender and I fold it in Jamie's blankets and smother him with the scent. Frost troops over the fields and I take the cold in great gulps. Gulps deep and smarting. For I'm trying to breathe in the place where the cold comes from—fox prints in snow, the white sprint of hares, and the mirrie dancers colouring the night. Peter finds me in the garden as the sky stirs between the yew trees. A feefle snow, I say. Our hands meet and we spin and spin. He unties my bonnet and the snowflakes fill my ringlets and then his hands are in my hair. After, we warm ourselves at the fire. The hall smells of holly and merriment. I rest my head on Peter's shoulder and he says the soft names he called me in the high places. Night settles in the windows. Stars peep from the yew trees. We will walk arm in arm to church at midnight and, after the prayers and lessons, we will sing Christmas all the way home.

Winter melts: the larks sing, hedgehogs scurry across the garden, snowdrops wilt, and Jamie crawls. He crawls to me, his face as round and rosy as an apple ready for biting, and I swoop him up and whirl him. When it's mizzling, I hold him to the window and point out the wrens with worms in their beaks and the blackbirds plucking moss. He chortles and it warms me. Peter tosses him in the air and catches him. We laugh louder than rain.

I hear something when Jamie crawls. A faint rustle. Not when Peter's reading him a story and stomping and fe fi fo fumming about the nursey. Not when the magpie is in the yew trees chattering like a clipmalabor. Only when all else is still and hush, I hear it - like the old pages of a book turned softly. I strain my ears. Jamie crawls to me. There it is again. I strip him and shake his clothes. But no paper falls out. He cries. He shakes his fists. I hear it again. I pry his chubby hands open, but they're empty and the smell of books wafts over me.

Can you hear it? I say. Peter closes the book of folk tales. Listen. I raise my finger. Jamie crawls and gurgles. What am I listening for? Peter tilts his head. Can't you hear it? He looks at me, his eyes dreich, and I want him to see me as he did in the high places. So, I take his hand and we stand at the window. A green rain is shaking the primroses. The air is thick with late Spring. A cloud breaks and the sun comes. I entwine my fingers in his and I tell him: Mam said Summer comes on a thousand silver slippered feet and you can hear them on the last day of May. He pulls me against him.

I don't listen. I keep the windows open to the roar of summer, even when a daggle rain bends the yew trees, even when a gos-elet rain bursts onto the floorboards. I sing until my voice bumps against the walls and I dance with my feet as heavy as I can make them and I fe fi fo fum louder than Peter. But still I hear the rustle. Even when Jamie turns in his sleep. Is it just my fancy? I used to dream of the bodach and weep myself awake. Mam pulled my ringlets off my face. She lit a lamp, and she threw salt in the hearth. But the shadows had its shape. I was half dream-ing. Perhaps, I'm half dreaming now?

Jamie rasps. And Peter hears. He hears before I tell him. For I thought it was my fancy, so I plugged my ears with summer sounds—bees and storms and the heat that swells like a song. The doctor comes and presses a stethoscope to Jamie's chest. He listens. Peter pulls me close. The room pauses. Normal, the Doctor says, and he blathers on about fresh air and warm drinks, but all I hear is Jamie rasping.

We spend whole days in the garden—out with the sparrows, in with the bats. When Jamie naps, I coorie him under the yew trees. The bench is warm and squirrels dart past my feet. He toddles on the path, his face an apple, but his voice gone. All gone. No gurgling. No chortling. Just rasping. Peter watches us from his study window. I call to him. He looks down. The heat is green and gold and sticky through my dress. Jamie swelters and cries, but he cries in rasps. I cover my ears. We stay outside until the stars and I carry him in asleep.

Peter paces through the night. I half sleep. I try to dream my way to wild places, away from gardens and walls. When I do slumber, I'm running through the frith, the deer forest, and the ferns are clinging to me. I wake to Jamie's cry—the rasping. Peter sits on the bed, his head in his hands. Why haven't you gone to him? I ask. He doesn't look up. I run to the nursery. Jamie's face is red. His hands are fists. I whisper to him and stroke his cheek. But his skin feels like paper. I snatch my hand back. Can't you shut him up? Peter stares at me. I shake my head. He grips Jamie's crib. His hands are white. Jamie rasps louder. And then his face flattens and pales and flattens and pales. I cry out. I try to grasp his fist, his chubby fist. It flattens in my hand. Jamie is paper. He flails his paper fists. What have you done? Peter staggers. I didn't. I didn't.

Jamie is paper. But he still toddles. He still cries. He reaches for his rattle but his paper hands bend. He can't hold it. I shake it for him. He makes a sound like laughter if laughter was paper. He smiles. I lift him gently so gently onto my lap. I can't coorie him for I will crumple him. My tears come and I turn my head, so I don't dampen him. I hear Peter and the doctor outside the door. It opens. The doctor's face falls. He says he will not return to this godless house. This is your doing, Peter says. You birthed him. He goes. The door slams. It's just us. Me and my bairn. But it isn't my doing. What is paper to do with me? What are books to do with me? If I had made Jamie change, he would have become a thing of the high places: rock and wind and sky.

I lift Jamie from my lap. I watch him toddle. I stroke his paper cheek. I leave the room. I will have him back again—chubby and damp and gurgling. I will coorie him again. I know how. I light a lamp and I carry it to the library. I stare at Peter's books. Books he held as if they were his bairns. He said there were too many to count. I try not to breathe in their musty stench. I smash the lamp. Flames burst and rush. I feel their heat. I watch them climb the shelves. I watch them gobble the books. Paper falls in burning flakes. I smell ash. I run. He will be him again. I open the door. I stagger. Jamie is paper. Flames crawl over him. Flames bite into him. He burns and burns.

Swallow It Down

Sarah Dropek

Sarah Dropek writes poetry and fiction
in Texas. Her work can be read in
Wyldblood Magazine, Mirror, Mirror:
A Compendium of Fractured Fairytales
from Fractured Mirror Publishing, and
HerStry. Her poetry can be read in Ink
Drinkers Poetry and Solana.

The first time Catherine almost did it was as she was brushing her mother's hair. Brianna, the home nurse Catherine had finally needed to hire, had left twenty minutes ago. The house was quiet without her chatter that usually filled the space left by her mother's silence. And in the stillness, Catherine's heart slowed to the shushing rhythm of the brush in her hands as she went through the motions of caregiving.

There wasn't a lot of hair left on her mother's head. And what remained was wiry, white, and stubbornly straight, even though Catherine had black and white photos that proved their hair had once been the same curly auburn. She wondered what age might take from her as the brush snagged at the nape of her mother's neck. Catherine gently pulled the tangle free and stared at the white strands held within it.

I should eat it.

Like the urge to water a drooping plant, the thought came from a place of such purity, it precluded any possible judgment. So, Catherine simply rolled the idea over in her mind like she would one of her mother's old strawberry candies on her tongue.

She pulled the strands from the brush and made one tight knot between them. And then another, and another, until she had a tiny, tense ball of hair in her palm. A morsel just waiting to be swallowed.

Her mother coughed and Catherine shoved the tidbit into her shirt pocket before threading the brush back through thinning strands. She finished quickly and began dinner. Except for the incessant hum of the air conditioner, the house was quiet as Catherine spooned plain pasta between her mother's thin lips.

To many it might have felt lonely, but Catherine preferred the silence since her mother had begun to deteriorate. It was a respite from the subtle sniping she had brought back into her life when her mother came to stay, along with the sickly-sweet scent of her aging skin.

For Catherine, silence had become a way of survival in such a loud world. At work, as she parsed through lines of code, she acquiesced to white noise in her headphones to tune out her just-barely adult colleagues regaling everyone with their weekend escapades. She understood the need for an open floor plan in her office, but desperately missed the plush fabric walls of her cubicle that filtered everything around her into cushioned echoes. And at home, the unignorable volume of her mother's judgments had finally ceased.

It was a Tuesday morning last year when her mother stopped speaking completely. Catherine had hired Brianna by then, and the nurse said she would have been worried except that her mother started writing. Pages and pages until her hand cramped and curled and she could no longer manage it.

Catherine had still not brought herself to read the diary, which Brianna insisted on leaving atop the coffee table as if her mother might start up again someday. She was scared the words inside would be a nonsensical jumble It was only after the small sips of whiskey Catherine allowed herself in the evenings when she would admit she was more terrified the diary would be perfectly understandable. That it held in its pages her mother's last indictment of all of Catherine's failures.

Unless I eat them.

It wasn't her own voice in her mind, barely even a voice at all. But as her mother's milky gaze watched Catherine mechanically lift the spoon to her mouth, she couldn't deny the thought was there. The moist sound of her mother's opening mouth only seemed to compel her more.

Once the bite was successfully masticated, Catherine stood from the table and went to the living room. The carpet had thinned, and her knees protested as she knelt down, but she didn't want her mother's incriminating eyes on her while she did it.

Her fingers hesitated over the diary. It looked like one of Brianna's daughter's cast-offs, with six puppies staring out from the cover on a grassy hill that could have been anywhere or nowhere at all. It was just the sort of nondescript image Catherine leaned on sometimes as filler while creating mock websites for clients.

She took in a small sip of air and opened to the first page.

'This is for you,' was all she read before closing the diary and staring once again at the puppies. For the briefest moment, Catherine entertained the thought that her mother had some sort of secret lover near the end and had written to them in her final moments of clarity. Maybe they, too, had been stricken down by age and couldn't make it to her ailing bedside. She almost opened the journal again to check.

But her hammering heart knew all that waited behind the set of six droopy eyes staring at her was more misunderstanding, disappointment, and spite. Her mother had tried her entire life to box

Catherine in, to cajole her into some semblance of the daughter she had imagined forty-eight years ago. Catherine wasn't going to let her last written words be burned into her mind like every other thing her mother had ever said about her. In fact, Catherine would make them disappear forever.

Without looking, she tore out the first page and pinched off little sections of paper. She put a few in her mouth and let them sit. There was a brief flash of brightness to the taste—Catherine imagined the pen ink melting over her tongue in thin black rivers—and then bland nothing. She was mostly surprised by how tough it was to chew, even after her spit hydrated the pieces. But she took her time, piercing the paper with her canines to try to wear the pieces down until she finally swallowed them all in little pulpy balls, each smaller than the tied ball of hair still safe in her pocket.

She leaned back against the couch and breathed in deeply. She swallowed again and felt a calm settle into her bones. Another deep breath, through her nose, slower. Yoga breathing, the girls at work would say. As Catherine breathed her deep inhales and slow exhales, she found, for the first time since her mother had moved in, she didn't mind the newer, mustier scent of her house as much when it hit her nose.

In fact, she more than didn't mind, she felt like she could finally breathe in this space that had become oppressive with her mother's belongings, lugged to and fro from each care facility until they had landed in her home.

She ate another handful of the diary, then a full page. She only stopped when she noticed the light had begun to fade through the windows. Her breath snagged, worried her mother might have died, quietly choking on a piece of food, slipping out of her chair and suffocating on the rug. She was sure the police would inexplicably know it was Catherine's negligence.

I can't be locked up before I eat the rest.

She dashed back into the kitchen from the short hall that led to the living room to find her mother sitting. Alive, fine. Maybe a bit grayer than before, but mostly the same.

The doctors had told her to expect a slow decline. One had even pulled her aside to relay an anecdote of his own parents, how it had felt like living with the dead. Catherine hadn't been able to decide if he had been fruitlessly, and rather inappropriately, flirting with her, or if he was being kind. Either way, he'd been right.

Her mother was in the chair in front of her, still very much breathing. But in the time it had taken Catherine to eat those first two pages, she'd seemed to slump more towards the ground, as if begging it to become her grave.

Catherine ate three more pages that night after her mother had been tucked safely in bed.

***

Brianna arrived just as Catherine was leaving for work the next morning.

"I made some extra coffee, please help yourself, Brianna," Catherine said as she gathered her phone and keys. She heard a lightness in her voice that mirrored her mood and liked the sound of it so much she kept talking. "Too much caffeine makes me shaky, so it's half-caff, but still a nice dark roast flavor!"

Brianna only smiled awkwardly.

"Mother and I stayed up a little late last night watching some of her old shows," Catherine continued, smiling to herself. "Hopefully she's not too difficult for you today."

A little white lie, but she wanted Brianna to like her. And it wasn't completely untrue. She had stayed up watching mother's old shows, it was just that her mother had been asleep already for hours when she did it. In the same way that eating the diary felt right, watching her mother's favorite sitcoms felt like some ritual she needed to go through to begin to say goodbye, to close the book on this person she wasn't sure she ever really had known after putting so much distance between them after childhood.

"That's...umm, really sweet," Brianna said, shuffling through her bags. "I'm sure it'll be fine. I'm sure she loved it. Have a good day."

"You too, Brianna. See you at six!" Catherine grinned before walking out into the heat of mid-summer, relishing the smell of the warm air baking the pavement and how her blouse clung to her skin.

She picked up donuts for the office and laughed at her coworkers' jokes over flaky sugar that she licked from her fingers. She felt new, reborn. Eating her mother's final words, unread, made her feel powerful. She was no longer the child, forced to listen. In erasing her mother's voice, she felt she was finally finding her own.

She rolled the ball of her mother's hair between her fingers while she worked, anxious to get home and finish what remained of the diary.

***

Brianna's face was flushed when Catherine pulled her keys from the lock.

"Everything alright?" Catherine chirped.

"It's Meggie... she's different today," was all Brianna said.

"Different good or different bad?" Catherine asked, holding her breath.

She was suddenly worried her mother would die before she had finished her strange goodbye and it made her blood burn, like it would steal away her newfound confidence. Her mother's last hurrah would be to beat Catherine to the punch.

"Different...scared?" Brianna squeaked. "I don't know. She just isn't responding the same. Her heart rate is high. I think she's been trying to speak, which she hasn't done for months. She should see her doctor."

Brianna stood by the door with her bag already slung over her shoulder. Her arms drew tightly across her chest and she chewed at her nail so hard that Catherine had to control the urge to swat at her hand and tell her to compose herself.

"Of course. I'll make the appointment, no need to worry. I'm sure it's just the heat," Catherine reassured her.

"Thanks," Brianna mumbled before flying out the door.

Catherine knew her mother would be seated comfortably at the table, ready for dinner, as Brianna always made sure to leave her. So she didn't bother looking in the kitchen to check on her before kneeling in front of the diary and carefully ripping out each page. As she did it, she stared at the upholstery of the sofa and decided it might be nice to redecorate when all this was over. She wondered when her taste had gotten so modern and austere as to have a white couch with unwelcoming teak armrests at each end. Once this was done, she wanted comfort, maybe even companionship again.

She boiled the pages with two quarts of water. As she watched them disintegrate back into the pulpy mess they came from, she thought it might be nice to add a little flavor to the final send off. In the end, she made a slightly thick, slightly too-sweet tea concoction, but it went down alright, and the taste reminded her of muggy evenings on the porch set to the tune of buzzing cicadas.

When the pot was almost empty, she began to feel like herself again. She pulled out the small ball of hair and popped it in her mouth. It smelled of shampoo and tasted strawberry sweet. She swallowed it down with the last sips of the diary.

Back in the kitchen, she regarded the lifeless body in the chair. It had gone ashen, with its age-curved spine hunched over a bowl of rice at the table. She caressed a sallow cheek, shuddered at the deep rivers of wrinkles on the skin. Pulling her thick curls into a bun, Meggie pushed away the panic of almost being lost to the dying shell.

No matter. The diary had finally done the trick. Catherine's weakness and insecurity had fed from its pages and let Meggie take hold.

Leaving the body to deal with in the morning, Meggie went to the kitchen to cook something with some flavor to it.

She would go for a walk tomorrow, visit Catherine's work and maybe find a date to the movies, take advantage of a life her daughter had squandered. But tonight was for celebrating, Meggie thought, as she pulled some ham from the fridge. She hummed a cheery tune and set Catherine's weak coffee leftovers to boil for a red-eye gravy that would rid the taste of her daughter's failures from her mouth.

THANK YOU TO OUR SUPPORTERS

Many thanks to our patrons and supporters, especially:

Johanna Levene • Wichael Tellez • Kate Boyes
Cathrin Hagey • Natalie Weizenbaum

Frederick Stark • Alina Kanaski • Jeffery Reynolds
Myz Lilith • D.M. Domosea • carol shoemake
Erik DeBill • Bonnie Warford • Felicia OSullivan
Salomao Becker • Anna O'Brien • Martin Cohen
J'nae Spano • Tory Hoke

Matthew Bennardo • Kayla • Lorna D Keach • smokestack
Lisa Short • Leslie Anderson • Sian Jones
Kristina Saccone • Rocky B • BethOfAus • J. Askew
Dirck de Lint • Brit Hvide • Wanda • Karen Anderson
Charlotte Nash-Stewart • Jocelyn Actual • Carly Racklin
Liz Warner • Suzanne Thackston • Jen G
Emily Anderson • Maria Haskins • GriffinFire

Want to see your name here? Become a patron!
patreon.com/lunastation

About the Cover Artist

Caroline Jamhour is a self-taught, independent artist from Brazil who works in both digital and traditional media. Having been drawn to fantasy and nature since childhood, her art explores the realms of the mythical and symbolic, seeking to express her own inner experiences. Through dark, dream-like imagery and mysterious characters, she offers glimpses into secret, liminal worlds.

www.carolinejamhour.com

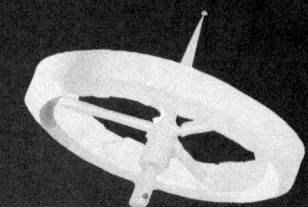

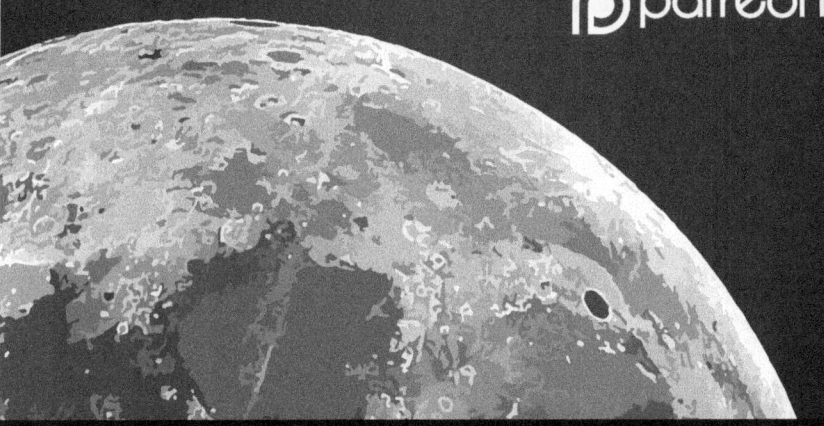